The
Genius Princ
Guide to Rais
a Nation Out of Debt
(Hey, How About Treason?)
Toru Toba
Illustration Falmaro
MW00464786
©Falmaro

©Falmaro
"You didn't need to come greet us at the door, Marquess of Marden."
Welcoming Wein's group into Elythro Palace was Zenovia, dressed to the nines in full regalia.

"I appreciate your coming all this way, Prince Wein."
Marquess of Marden
Zenovia

It was as if he
was suggesting it
was no big deal
to disavow their
natural rights as
royalty. Hearing
Wein's comment
made Zeno assume
a look of surprise.

©Falmaro
"——Ngh!"
Zeno

"Welcome, young prince."
King of Soljest Kingdom
Gruyere

©Falmaro
Princess of Soljest Kingdom
Tolcheila
“I’ve been curious to find out more about the rumored ‘Prince Wein’.”

CONTENTS

The Genius Prince's Guide to Raising a Nation Out of Debt (Hey, How About Treason?)

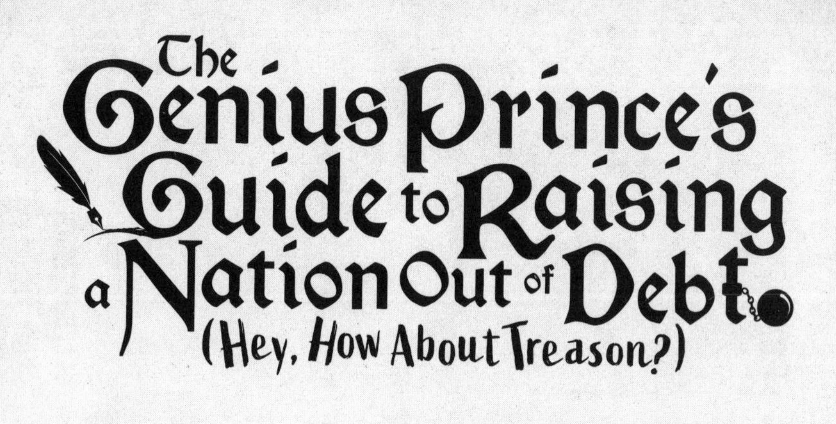

Toru Toba
Illustration Falmaro

New York

The Genius Prince's Guide to Raising a Nation Out of Debt (Hey, How About Treason?)

Toru Toba

Translation by Jessica Lange
Cover art by Falmaro

This book is a work of fiction. Names, characters, places, and incidents are the product of the author's imagination or are used fictitiously. Any resemblance to actual events, locales, or persons, living or dead, is coincidental.

Original Japanese edition published in 2019 by SB Creative Corp.

This English edition is published by arrangement with SB Creative Corp., Tokyo in care of Tuttle-Mori Agency, Inc., Tokyo.

Yen On
150 West 30th Street, 19th Floor
New York, NY 10001

Visit us at yenpress.com
facebook.com/yenpress
twitter.com/yenpress
yenpress.tumblr.com
instagram.com/yenpress

First Yen On Edition: December 2020

Yen On is an imprint of Yen Press, LLC.
The Yen On name and logo are trademarks of Yen Press, LLC.

The publisher is not responsible for websites (or their content) that are not owned by the publisher.

Library of Congress Cataloging-in-Publication Data
Names: Toba, Toru, author. | Falmaro, illustrator. | Lange, Jessica (Translator), translator.
Title: The genius prince's guide to raising a nation out of debt (hey, how about treason?) / Toru Toba ; illustration by Falmaro ; translation by Jessica Lange.
Other titles: Tensai ouji no akaji kokka saisei-jyutsu, souda, baikoku shiyou. English
Description: First Yen On edition. | New York, NY : Yen On, 2019-
Identifiers: LCCN 2019017156| ISBN 9781975385194 (v. 1 : pbk.) | ISBN9781975385170 (v. 2 : pbk.) | ISBN 9781975309985 (v. 3 : pbk.) | ISBN 9781975310004 (v. 4 : pbk.) | ISBN 9781975313708 (v. 5 : pbk.)
Subjects: LCSH: Princes—Fiction.
Classification: LCC PL876.O25 T4613 2019 | DDC 895.6/36—dc23
LC record available at https://lccn.loc.gov/2019017156

ISBNs: 978-1-9753-1370-8 (paperback)
978-1-9753-1371-5 (ebook)

10 9 8 7 6 5 4 3 2 1

LSC-C

Printed in the United States of America

The Genius Prince's Guide to Raising a Nation Out of Debt (Hey, How About Treason?)

NORTH SEA
THE GIANT'S BACKBONE
KINGDOM OF NATRA
CODEBELL
Royal Capital
PHITHCHA
MARDEN
Principality of Marden
KINGDOM OF SOLJEST
THOLITUKE
THE GIANT'S BACKBONE
KINGDOM OF CAVARIN
KINGDOM OF DELUNIO
TORYSTORIA

Chapter 1 | Hey, How About Feeding My Massive Ego?

Summers in Natra were markedly short.

There was a geographic explanation for this: its location at the northernmost end of the continent.

The warm season made people buzz with activity, and the Kingdom of Natra was no exception. Because summers never lasted long, the citizens were bent on making the most of every minute. In fact, they seemed to come more alive than any other nation.

On top of that, they were humming with excitement over the various exploits of Prince Wein. All had expected this summer to be particularly spirited, and they weren't wrong.

... Except this year had an element of surprise.

The season drew to a close. Fall was just around the corner.

It was the time of year to cool off their heated heads, but the citizens of the kingdom were continuing to party like it was midsummer.

There was one reason for it.

The Kingdom of Natra was flourishing.

"—Heh-heh-heh-heh."

An eerie chuckle echoed through the room.

It held an uncontainable mirth that seemed to spill out involuntarily.

©Falmaro

"Ha-ha-ha-ha… Ha-ha-ha-ha!"

After a short fit, the peals of laughter became louder and louder.

"HA-HA-HA-HA-HA—*gh?! Koff!*"

Wrong pipe. After a few seconds of violent coughing, someone softly sighed.

"Oof… I should've known better than to do that without practice."

A boy was massaging his throat.

The Crown Prince of the Kingdom of Natra. Wein Salema Arbalest.

"—But let me give it another go!"

"Stop."

A stack of papers smacked the top of his head before he could go for round two.

Wein turned around to find his aide, Ninym Ralei, hovering over him.

"Why strain your vocal cords for nothing?"

They were in his office at Willeron Palace. The gentle breeze blowing through the open window signaled autumn was coming.

"I can't think of anything more embarrassing than a prince laughing himself hoarse."

"…You've got a point." Wein offered the tiniest nod. "But this doesn't happen every day! I think I can afford to get a little hyped!"

"I hear you, but…"

He was talking about Natra's recent windfall.

The documents on his desk marked the traffic of incoming goods and people, as well as resulting business dealings and anticipated revenue. All signs pointed to their economy on the up-and-up.

"Increased revenue and profits! And room to keep growing! How could I not laugh? Let's ditch our political duties and party!"

"Seeing the world through rose-colored glasses, huh…"

The Kingdom of Natra was notorious for sucking on three major levels: location, industry, and reputation. A triple threat, but in the worst way.

There was one reason why it had suddenly caught a break: It had managed to shed its suckiness.

How did this happen?

First, location. Two hundred years ago, the nation had been founded on prime restate, which could be attributed to its relations with one of the biggest religions in the Western continent—the Teachings of Levetia.

According to doctrine, its founder had made a loop around Varno upon receiving a divine message from God, tracing the entire continent from west to north to east to south, before circling back to the West.

It was only a matter of time before the trail became a pilgrimage. The Kingdom of Natra had been founded on its route, serving as a continental divide nestled deep in the northern mountains. It didn't take long for it to become a hotspot for potential business dealings with followers of Levetia.

Which was how we were able to thrive in the past, Ninym reminded herself.

However, a hundred years after their founding, the situation had been flipped on its head, due to the Circulous Law. Based on a new interpretation of the scriptures, a half loop around the western section of the continent was now considered an acceptable pilgrimage.

This had been a huge blow for Natra.

Many chose to take the new route that circumvented the nation, since it was shorter and safer. As a result, the number of people passing through their kingdom dropped drastically. Once a necessary pit stop for traveling believers, the Kingdom of Natra had been downgraded to the middle of nowhere in an instant.

And we finally had a beacon of light this spring.

One hundred years since the implementation of the Circulous Law, the neighboring kingdom—Marden—had vowed allegiance to Natra. Obviously, this was going to boost Natra's power as a nation, and more important, Marden was on the new pilgrimage route. Their union meant Natra had gotten a piece of good real estate for the first time in a hundred years.

Not that this will restore our former glory.

This left them with two other problems: no viable industries and a crappy reputation.

Marden hadn't taken advantage of the stream of people passing through the kingdom. After all, it had nothing to offer.

In fact, the two nations were on par when it came to the infertility of their land and the lack of basic infrastructure to accommodate travelers and their companions.

That said, they couldn't just offer imported goods from other nations in the West, since the travelers would be hitting up those exact spots as they completed their pilgrimage. They could have attempted to bring in goods from the East, though that trade route had been blockaded by Natra.

At first glance, this problem could have been resolved by the two nations joining forces. However, Natra had distanced itself from other kingdoms after it was forcibly ejected from the route, and Marden hadn't wanted to associate with Natra, fearing animosity from Levetia.

But our union has settled this dilemma.

Their own industries were as lousy as ever. However, their alliance with Earthworld Empire had allowed them to import goods from the other half of the continent for the past hundred years.

In other words, they could offer the hottest commodities of the East.

As for reputation, that's been addressed by Wein and Princess Falanya.

Even with the best goods and location, a terrible reputation was enough to keep people away.

Though his recent exploits were outstanding, Prince Wein had been only a topic of local discussion until the previous year. The citizens under his care and government leaders in other nations were in the know, but residents of other kingdoms weren't too familiar with the intimate details.

"I've heard that one prince is doing okay for himself," someone would say.

"Cool," another would offer.

However, his approach to the incident in the merchant city of Mealtars had certainly changed things. Every influential leader from each nation had been there, and the event had drawn the attention of the entire continent. Everyone across Varno knew the names of Prince Wein and Princess Falanya, now that they'd come in clutch at the eleventh hour.

Inevitably, it boosted their reputation as a whole, recognized in the eyes of society.

Now the Kingdom of Natra became a triple threat of the good kind: prime real estate, covetable goods, stellar reputation. As a result, the winds of fortune blew down on them for the first time in a hundred years.

"Whew! It ain't easy being a genius!"

With everything that had happened, Wein's ego had inflated to grand proportions. If his ballooning self-importance could take up space in the real world, there would be enough room for him to do a little jig on it.

To make things worse for Ninym, it wasn't wrong to attribute these recent successes to his ingenuity in the face of adversity. She couldn't make up her mind to admonish or agree with him.

"If we continue to flourish, the people will be happy, and our budget will get even bigger! Which means more opportunities will present themselves to us! And that'll let us live in the lap of luxury! Our value as a kingdom will climb! Smooth sailing from here on out! Yes, ma'am! I think I'll keep living the high life as a prince!"

"...Says the one who was eager to commit treason and retire. Changing your tune, huh."

"What?! Retire? Commit treason? Who said that? I'm only committed to upholding this position and indulging in extravagance!"

"I'm relieved to hear that. Enjoy." A mountain of paperwork landed on his desk. "I need you to look over and sign these reports from each department. This one wants to know if we'd like to import additional dyes from the Empire. This says they're low on personnel at the border and request a bigger budget. And a letter of protest has arrived from the Delunio Kingdom, so please write back to them."

"...Why do I have more responsibilities now that we're doing well, Miss Ninym?!"

"Because it means more people and more jobs. And that leads to more paperwork for those in charge."

"I knew it! I have to sell off this kingdom and get out of here...!"

He was never one to hesitate to turn his back on his people.

"Wein, I swear..." She looked positively beat. "Well, I guess it's too late to correct your personality. Whatever. There's something we need to resolve immediately. And it's not paperwork."

"Hmm?!" Wein scoffed. "Fine! Good times don't necessarily mean fewer responsibilities! But you can't be seriously suggesting there's an irresolvable problem! I mean, do you know who you're talking to? There's no way that's the case! After all, where there's work, there's money! And money can solve anything! That's the distinct pleasure of being king! Ha-ha-ha! I wish I knew what it's like to feel defeated!"

"All right. I'll give it a try. What are you going to do about our new territory—Marden?"

Wein stopped signing papers. His ego deflated until he collapsed onto his desk.

There was a moment of silence.

"...Ninym."

"Yes?"

"You know, there's a bitter taste to defeat..."

"That was easy." Ninym sighed in exasperation. "So, what are you going to do?"

"AAAAAAH!" he shouted in agony. "Aaah! Jeez! What am I supposed to do with Marden?!"

"This is a tricky one..." She had on a look of concern as Wein clutched his head.

Who would benefit the most from economy expansion in Natra?

Marden, of course. Of the three threats, its territory boasted a location for people to gather and conduct business.

Since Marden was part of their kingdom, any boost to its economy carried over to Natra. That meant nothing was amiss...except that wasn't how things worked in a feudal system.

"If we can keep this boom going, it won't even take ten years before Marden will surpass the Arbalest family."

Yikes, Wein thought, scrunching up his face.

In a feudal state composed of many lords, it was necessary to maintain national power to remain at the top. With it came the ability to mobilize soldiers—and this was an era where military power was paramount.

That is to say, any leader without national power would be considered weak. Without the people's support, the other lords would distance themselves.

"Of course," Ninym continued, "it's a big 'if.' Realistically speaking, I imagine we'll have to deal with some form of interference and sabotage."

"But let's say nothing changes. In ten years, Marden will stop listening to us… Guess we better do something about it."

In history, there were certainly kings who retained control with their popularity and charisma, despite having less power than their lords. However, these were exceptions.

"It'd be nice if we'd just have to deal with insubordination. I mean, they used to be royals, and now they're under our thumb. They're all going to be a little stubborn, including the citizens and Zenovia."

Zenovia was the lord in charge of Marden. As the former princess of the royal family, she was appointed to marquess after swearing vassalage to Natra.

"Do you think she'll betray us, Wein?"

In the past, she had concealed her identity when she accompanied Wein on his journey to Cavarin. He'd witnessed her sincerity firsthand, but…

"It's possible," he replied, nodding. "Zenovia and Marden are joined at the hip. If it's for her former nation, she isn't above launching sneak attacks or stabbing us in the back."

"True. I mean, her allegiance was essentially a sneak attack."

"See? And in the realm of politics, her vassals might pressure her into something. If it were me, I would plan to break away ASAP. This is just a fire waiting to happen."

Marden was a new addition to Natra with enough clout to give the Arbalest family a run for its money. Many of the lords in Wein's kingdom were wary of this territory.

For foreign spies, this was a golden opportunity. It was almost too easy to sow discord between Marden and the old guard of Natra, get them to attack each other, then go in for the kill once the two sides had worn themselves out.

What could they do about it?

"The heart of the issue stems from the surrounding regions. They can't keep up with the rapid growth of Marden, which has led to some concerns that this economic gap will just keep widening," Wein explained. "In other words, if we all grow at the same rate, we'll be able to keep hold of the situation."

"Makes sense. But how will you go about it?"

"Funny you should ask." Wein snorted. "I've got nothing!"

Ninym massaged her temples.

"What did you expect me to do? If I had a magic spell to solve everything, I would have used it already!"

He was right, but she still frowned. "...But without it, our future looks bleak."

"I knooow! Urgh! I wanted to savor this moment! Why can't the problems just wait a little? You know, read the room!" Wein groaned. "Rrrrgh!"

Ninym looked at him from the corner of her eye, thinking aloud.

"Let's see... What if you slowed down their boom and limited foreign business deals to stunt Marden's growth?"

That would decelerate their development and effectively close the gap, but...

"No way!"

"I knew it."

It might nip one problem in the bud, but it would come at the cost of their current success.

"In that case, we *could* find business partners outside of Marden."

Ninym was right. If they could profit from other clients, it would prevent Marden from being the only region rising at a breakneck pace.

"Question is, who? Do we even have anyone who would be interested in doing business with us?"

"Yeah..." Ninym groaned, crossing her arms. Wein followed suit.

Someone knocked on the door. An official walked in.

"Pardon me, Your Highness. An emissary has arrived from Soljest Kingdom."

"From Soljest?"

Wein and Ninym exchanged a look. Soljest was one of the nations that bordered Marden. Their king, Gruyere, was one of the Holy Elites.

"Yes. What shall I do?"

"...Tell them I'm coming. Show them to the reception room."

"Understood." The official retreated.

Ninym cocked her head to the side. "Soljest, huh... Maybe King Gruyere has something important he wants to discuss? Hey, Wein... Wein?"

She turned to him when he didn't reply. Reflecting in her red pupils was his broad smile.

"—I've got a plan."

Tholituke. Former capital of the Kingdom of Marden. Current capital of the Marden marquisate.

Elythro Palace had once been home to royalty. It now served as an administrative facility after undergoing major renovations.

It used to reflect the garish taste of King Fyshtarre and be known for serving no practical use. It had almost burned completely to the ground when Cavarin had attacked.

Even though it was an impractical edifice, it was still considered a symbol of the royal capital. Once the people reclaimed the land from Cavarin, they made plans to rebuild it as an administrative building, making sure it fit the budget and prioritizing functionality.

A man hurried down the new hallway.

Known as Jiva, he was distinctly round, serving originally as a diplomat of the Kingdom of Marden. He had joined the Liberation Army after the capital fell, and his patriotism and honest nature had won Zenovia's trust. With the capital back in their hands, he now served as her right-hand man.

Jiva arrived at one of the palace offices. He caught his breath for a moment before knocking on the door. Someone groaned inside.

"I knew it..."

With a troubled expression, he opened the door, but he stopped before he stepped inside. A piece of paper had fallen in front of his feet.

When he looked up, he realized the entire floor was littered with documents and other reference materials. In fact, there was nowhere for him to stand. He started to pick up the papers at his feet, peering at the desk farther back in the room.

There was someone predictably planting their face on its surface.

"Lady Zenovia, please wake up. Lady Zenovia...!"

"Nngh..."

Rousing at his call, a young woman slowly peeled herself from the desk. Her hair was mussed from sleep. Wrinkles from the papers marked her face.

She was the master of the palace, former princess of Marden, and current marquess of Natra.

Zenovia.

"Oh...hello, Jiva. Is it morning already?" She looked at him through sleepy eyes.

"Hello? No time for hellos...!" Jiva reprimanded. "Did you pull

an all-nighter reading papers again? I believe I've requested you sleep in your bedroom."

"Yes, but…there was a section that was bothering me…"

"How many times will you use this excuse? And your hair… It's quite something."

Jiva looked exasperated as he beckoned more people from beyond the door. Ladies-in-waiting began to file in.

"Please draw a bath for Lady Zenovia."

"Understood."

"Ah, but I'm still in the middle of reading the papers from yesterday."

"No 'buts.' You have a meeting today, and that necessitates you dressing up. What will your vassals think if you appear before them in your current state?"

The ladies-in-waiting started to drag Zenovia off to her bath as she received a scolding from Jiva.

He sighed.

A third party ventured to make a comment.

"—I've gotten used to seeing Lady Zenovia get hauled off."

The speaker was a man in his prime. Based on his muscular body and clothing, it didn't take more than one glance to realize he was someone from the military.

"Borgen, are you here to deliver your usual reports to Lady Zenovia?"

"Yeah. Bad timing, it seems. Ha-ha-ha."

"This is no laughing matter, Borgen," Jiva said to the man, shaking his head. "She's destroying her body. Besides, we mustn't forget she's been forced into this position because we lack the competence to support her."

"Ngh, you have a point. My bad," Borgen replied, bowing his head.

He was one of the generals who had served Marden when it had still been a kingdom.

Borgen and Jiva went far back, and his archery skills were said to be the finest in the territory. Soldiers revered him as a man with a backbone, but that was also why he never got along with King Fyshtarre, which had landed him a post that left a lot to be desired.

After the capital fell, Borgen joined the Liberation Army led by Zenovia at Jiva's request. As a military commander with real experience, he was currently serving alongside Jiva as one of the top leaders of the territory.

"In any case, Marden will not last in its current state without her to lead us. I wish she could focus on studying governmental affairs, but…"

"King Fyshtarre shunned her as much as he did me…"

Zenovia didn't have any skills to write home about when it came to national politics. It would be a bit unfair to say this was due to her own willful negligence.

Born a prince, Wein had spent years receiving the education to rule as a monarch. On the other hand, Zenovia had been sent off to a villa away from the king, receiving virtually no education in politics. In other words, she lacked skill only because she hadn't spent much time acquiring it.

This explained why she was trying to pick up the pace by studying government while simultaneously running it.

"As vassals, we should be supporting Lady Zenovia, especially now, but…"

"Still having trouble rounding up more people, Jiva?"

"Things don't look too promising, though I guess I shouldn't have expected otherwise."

There just wasn't enough human capital in Marden for it to resume operations.

After all, they'd been to hell and back. Their former king had abused his power. They'd lost a war with Natra. Launched by Cavarin, a surprise attack had swiped their capital from under their noses, and the liberation army had locked swords with their new rulers. They'd banded with Natra to reclaim their land, only for their former princess to promptly swear allegiance to their temporary ally.

This had been a disorienting rush of events for the residents of the territory. What misfortune would the new day bring? Even for those in positions of power, it was hard to say if they were making the right decision by serving this new government.

"And there's still discord between those who left and those who stayed, even among the officers of the former kingdom." Jiva's expression turned dour.

During their short rule over Marden, Cavarin had tried to keep officials of this nation under their employ. As a result, these bureaucrats were left with three options: serve their new rulers, resist by joining the Liberation Army, or find another job altogether.

After Marden was freed, those in the Liberation Army were obviously the ones who gained distinction. Jiva and Borgen were appointed as chief leaders, and others were given distinguished positions within the territory. Those who hung around in Marden were called the "Remainers."

Things were harder for those who chose to serve Cavarin. With the death of their new king and hints of political upheaval in their new home, they were starting to jump ship again, taking advantage of the revival in Marden to sneak back. However, the Remainers were cold toward these so-called "Returners." From their perspective, they had tried to waltz back in after readily ditching their homeland.

"I guess accepting the Returners was a mistake? I can't stand watching soldiers bicker, much less civil officers."

"There was no way around it. They have critical insight into operating the territory. We'd be in over our heads if we pushed them away. We can't even find the people to train from the ground up. And we just don't have the time."

Borgen sighed. "Damn. We really can't catch a break. I thought this was going to be the best time of my life, but here I am, thinking fondly of the time when shit was boring but easy."

"Please don't step down. I know my assessment might have been wrong, but we'd be done without you."

"I know. I see Lady Zenovia working hard, even though she's twenty years younger than me. I would never forgive myself if I just abandoned her."

This was all that was keeping Marden together: vassals banding together under Zenovia, inspired by her work ethic, though she was sorely inexperienced.

It was the reason she had to stand before them, cheer them on, and act as an emotional pillar. Without her, the territory would fall to pieces.

"Besides, I can feel something in the air has changed since our economy improved. If we can get past this, I'm sure the world will be our oyster."

Borgen was in charge of patrolling and supervising the territory. He was intimately familiar with the impact this had on people's lives.

Jiva's expression remained grave. "So things have shifted in our favor. But that brings the problem of surrounding areas in Natra."

"Hm…I see your point. If Marden is the only one with new wealth, it could breed some animosity there. Especially since we're new to their kingdom."

"Precisely. Therefore—" Jiva stopped mid-sentence.

Zenovia had appeared down the hallway with her ladies-in-waiting.

"I'm back!"

No time had passed. She must have taken the quickest dip in the world.

It didn't seem she'd spent much time getting dressed either. Her ladies-in-waiting fussed over her dress and attempted to wipe her dripping hair. Zenovia was too old to be doing this. Jiva looked to the heavens for help.

"Lady Zenovia…I believe I've mentioned that appearing before the vassals in this state is—"

"Don't worry. I was sneaky in getting here."

"That's not the problem…!"

Storming after her, Jiva tried to give her a piece of his mind as they reentered the office.

Borgen interrupted. "Come on, Jiva. No need to raise your voice. She obviously can't rest with things on her mind. If you care about her health, it would be better to help her finish her tasks than keep her from them."

"Hmph…" Jiva groaned.

"Yeah. Tell him," Zenovia said under her breath.

He whipped around to glare at her. She looked away, feigning innocence.

Jiva sighed. "…Fine. I'll overlook it this time."

"And next time?"

"There will be no next time," he snapped.

Zenovia pouted before turning to Borgen.

"All right, Borgen. Let's hear your report."

"Please take a look at this." He handed her a sheaf of documents.

She thumbed over them as she sank in her chair. They contained information obtained during the patrol rounds.

"Seems turmoil in our territory has subsided."

"Yes. You were right to prioritize things to get the citizens to feel at peace. With the economy improving, it seems that has finally come to fruition."

"I wasn't sure how it would turn out, but it's one thing off my plate."

Zenovia couldn't stop herself from breaking out into a smile, but it didn't take long before she reined it back in.

"But being inattentive could lead to our downfall. Right, Jiva?"

"Yes. You're correct." He nodded. "If we continue to experience explosive growth, Natra won't keep quiet. That could spell trouble for both of us."

"...Which means we'll have to sit down with them at some point."

"About that. One of their emissaries has just arrived. They entrusted me with correspondence from Prince Wein."

"From the prince?" Zenovia accepted the sealed letter from Jiva, giving it a once-over.

She was floored by its contents.

"It says His Highness plans to pay us a visit... Is this true?"

"Yes. We've received verbal confirmation from the emissary. It seems Prince Wein has been invited to attend a ceremony in Soljest. Since Marden is on his route there, he wishes to talk with us."

"...And I don't assume he's coming to see the sights."

"Right. I imagine he's concerned about the friction between our two territories and wants to discuss it further."

"That works for us. Jiva, prepare to receive them. Borgen, make sure the prince is guarded during his stay."

"Yes!"

"As you wish."

They bowed to her. Zenovia nodded at them before looking like she'd remembered something and springing to her feet.

"Where are you going, Lady Zenovia?" Jiva inquired.

"...I might take a long soak in the bath after all," she replied awkwardly.

Something about her reaction was enough for him to understand. He nodded, smiling.

"I think that's a great idea. We'll take over your administrative duties. Please enjoy yourself to your heart's content."

"R-right. Well then, I'll leave it to you." Zenovia hurried out of the room.

Only the two remained. Borgen tilted his head and looked at Jiva. "What was that about?"

Jiva chuckled. "Lady Zenovia hasn't completely abandoned her maidenly side. She can't let herself look unsightly before Prince Wein."

I see. Borgen smiled in understanding. "Well, we've got our hands full as our precious gem polishes herself."

"Yes... But what are we going to do about this?" Jiva held out a separate sealed envelope.

"Another letter? Why didn't you give it to Lady Zenovia?"

"Well, the sender might pose a little problem..."

Borgen could tell from his loaded statement that they weren't on good terms. He asked a follow-up question.

"Who's it from?"

Jiva's eyes narrowed. "The Kingdom of Delunio."

Late summer. Their stage was set in the North.

Three nations had announced their arrival: Natra. Soljest. Delunio.

In the vast northern lands, three kingdoms were quietly scheming to engage in a brutal battle.

Chapter 2 | Visitors

"Hey, Claudius. Do you know about Soljest?"

This question had come from Wein's little sister, the princess of Natra—Falanya Elk Arbalest.

With her textbook within arm's reach, she had turned toward an elderly man standing nearby—Claudius. Her tutor.

"Of course," he replied, nodding politely. "It's a powerful nation with a militant army and rich culture. You'd be hard pressed to find anyone from the West who isn't familiar with Soljest."

"It's ruled by one of the Holy Elites, King Gruyere. What's he like?"

"I have not looked upon him myself, but he's known as the biggest glutton on the continent. There's no shortage of food-related rumors surrounding his personage. 'The Pig King lives off pork.' 'Capable of devouring half the nation.' 'The only things infinite are God's love and his appetite.'"

"Half the nation..."

"Do you remember the ceremony from the other day? It used to be a ritual to give thanks to the nation's bounty. This changed once King Gruyere ascended to the throne. I hear the royal capital spends this time gorging themselves and relishing in every culinary delight on the continent."

"Oh gosh..." Falanya put on a pained smile.

She was imagining a giant, intoxicated by the party spirit, clutching the entire city, ready to cram it into its gaping mouth.

"Of course, his appetite isn't his only trait. He's been king for over twenty years. One glance at their wealth serves as proof of his political prowess."

Claudius thumbed through the textbook in his hand, looking at a map of the area around Natra. It included Marden and Soljest in the West.

"Their kingdom has always had a warm-water port, allowing it to build its fortune through trade with foreign nations. Since the start of his reign, that harbor has gotten bigger, expanding their imports. And when it comes to war, he's achieved victory by personally leading his men to battle."

Claudius continued. "Though he's particular about his food, he is generous and admired by his subjects. Anyone would agree he's a wise ruler."

"That's impressive…" Falanya marveled, sighing with wonder.

It was easy to run a kingdom to ruin, but hard work to get it to flourish.

Even though she was young, she understood King Gruyere had to be a big deal if he could maintain a golden age for twenty years after ascending to the throne.

"So that's where Wein will be going…" Falanya thought for a moment. "Do you think they want to be our ally?"

"Could be," Claudius replied, nodding. "Even if it's not for an alliance, their kingdom might want to show an interest in developing friendly relations with surrounding nations. After all, they'd been fighting against Delunio since King Gruyere rose to power."

The Kingdom of Delunio was another nation in the West, situated next to Marden. Located southwest of Marden and south of Soljest, Delunio had had a rocky relationship with Soljest for decades.

"I've heard Marden had been called to facilitate between the two nations when it was still independent. Now that it's a part of Natra, Soljest might be hoping we'll take over the role. The logical step would be to reach out first and curry our favor."

"...Makes sense. If Natra and Delunio ended up on friendly terms and formed an alliance, that would spell trouble for Soljest." Falanya nodded.

Claudius broke into a smile.

"Hmm? What is it, Claudius?"

"Oh. Pay me no mind... It seems you've gotten a lot out of the incident in Mealtars. You've grown, Princess Falanya."

"Really?" She looked down at her own body. "I suppose I did get a little taller..." She scrunched up her face to scrutinize this change.

He gazed at her with soft eyes. Though she couldn't see it for herself, those in her inner circle had picked up on this development. Once childish and unreliable, Falanya had grown a spine since her return from Mealtars.

"You never used to be interested in foreign affairs, Princess. But you've been taking your studies very seriously to support Prince Wein. It's proof of your physical and mental maturity. Very impressive."

"R-really?" Falanya blushed upon receiving praise from her strict tutor.

Claudius wasn't finished. "Which is why I must tell you something."

His gaze sharpened. Falanya straightened her spine.

He faced her and spoke slowly. "Since the incident in Mealtars, many people on this continent have become aware of your name. The citizens toast to you. The vassals are moved by your growth. It has shown to the world that there's someone on equal footing with Prince Wein in Natra."

"What…? I can't possibly compare to my brother."

"Please pardon my rudeness. I must agree. Your abilities and achievements are far from those of Prince Wein. The citizens know this. But their perspective will change as you make more progress."

"…"

She understood what he was implying. If she continued to make great strides, they might insist she was on the same level as Wein.

So what?

Is it necessarily a bad thing to be praised for being on the same level as my brother? If I can prove myself, I can take off a load off his back. If he collapsed again like back in Mealtars, then I—

She suddenly realized something—comprehending what it meant to step in for the prince.

The blood drained from her face.

"You're right, Princess Falanya," Claudius said. "Prince Wein is slanted to be the future king… But as you become more famous, I imagine there will be those saying you are better suited to inherit the throne."

"That's ridiculous!" Falanya shouted. "Wein will be the next king. For anyone to think I would take that from him…!"

"I understand. I know your feelings and your bond with your brother. Consider it nothing more than a joke in poor taste. But," he continued, "the founder, Salema, and his older brother, Galea, were unable to escape the battle over inheritance, though they were known for being close."

"…Ngh."

Salema and Galea were princes of the former nation of Naliavene. The factions for both sides had bloated out of control. In the end, Salema abandoned his homeland to establish Natra.

"...Did I overstep boundaries? Should I have sat out even though Wein was in trouble?"

Falanya had stumbled on her way to help him, cursing herself for her own powerlessness. It was nothing like her days as a pampered princess. It had been grueling work, but she thought it had given her insight into the political realm.

However, if it came at the cost of the detriment of Wein and Natra, she had played the part of a fool.

Claudius tried to squash her worries. "Never. As the continent has started to experience unrest, your support was critical... Indispensable, even."

"But..."

"Think of it as the good of the nation, Princess Falanya," he continued. "From here on out, I'm sure there will be people drawn to your fame and attempt to earn your favor. Do not be moved by their words. Follow your own judgment and support Prince Wein. That is your next trial."

"My trial..."

The memory of her delivering a speech in Mealtars flashed in her mind. She'd never been so nervous. "Trial" seemed to be an appropriate word—and she had managed to overcome it.

...More roadblocks lie ahead, even though this is done...

And they would continue for the rest of her life.

Her esteemed brother had managed to overcome his fair share of challenges. She couldn't let one successful trial get to her head as his little sister.

"I'll do it," she said after a long pause. "I can't just sit by and do nothing. I'll support my brother and this nation."

She turned to Claudius.

"As payback for making me worry, I'll make you help me out."

©Falmaro

Claudius flashed her a look of shock, but it didn't take long for him to break into a smile and bow.

"And I shall do my best to serve Your Highnesses and Natra."

She shifted her gaze to the window. The western sky reflected in her eyes.

Somewhere under the same sky was her brother. She wondered how he was doing.

"Ngh…"

On the main road to Tholituke in Marden.

Protected on all sides by guards and his retinue, the carriage swayed forward. Inside, Wein had let out a troubled moan.

The source of his consternation was the cards in his hand. Across from him, Ninym clutched on to her set. They were passing the time with games until they reached their destination.

Based on their expressions, Wein was at a disadvantage. After all, his mind was elsewhere. As to why—

"This isn't the first time. Why do you care about it so much?" Ninym ran her fingers through her hair, looking exasperated.

The strands were black. She'd dyed it again, since they were traveling through the West.

"*Please* let me touch it."

"I said no. The color will rub out."

"Pretty please? Don't I have princely privileges?"

"No."

"Aww. Come on." Wein sulked, drawing another card from the deck.

His eyed widened a little bit.

"…How about if I win?"

"Must have been a good card." She broke into a sarcastic smile.

He was being almost too obvious. Ninym knew things could get ugly if she gave him the cold shoulder.

"Fine… But if I win, I get to dye *your* hair."

"My hair? What's so fun about that?" Wein fiddled with his bangs, tilting his head to the side.

Ninym looked like this was her best idea yet.

"Everything. I have a feeling this will be good. No one is forcing you, but if you say no, my hair is off-limits, too."

"Hmm…" He peeked at his hand before looking back at her. "You're on."

"We have a deal, then. Okay. Let's show each other our hands on three. One… Two… Three… Go."

Wein was mentally chuckling to himself.

—Heh, I've got you, Ninym!

While he'd distracted her with his bangs, he'd used his other hand to swap out his cards with the ones he needed in the discard pile.

I'm holding the second-best set of cards! I didn't have the cards to make the hand with the highest possible value, but I just discarded the card she needs to win! In other words, this battle is—

"I win."

"WHAAAAAT?!" Wein let out a shriek as he witnessed the perfect hand before his eyes.

"W-wait, Miss Ninym! How did you do that?!"

"By drawing cards, obviously. But I won't tell you from where."

"Gweh."

In other words, Ninym had switched her card for the one he'd just swapped out.

"I think I remember seeing your cards in the discard pile, Wein."

"Y-yeah? Are you sure your memory isn't playing tricks on you, Miss Ninym?"

"Whatever. I still win."

"AAAAAAH!"

Wein was getting the bitter taste of defeat. Next to him, Ninym seemed gleeful as she took out dyes from an unknown source.

"The quality could be better, but we have a whole range of colors. Hmm… Black… White… Blond… Do you have a preference?"

"Whatever you want… Oh, maybe not blond. That would make me stick out like a sore thumb."

"Blond it is."

"Didn't you just hear me?!"

"I think it'll look good on you."

It was the demand of a victorious tyrant. As the loser, Wein had no choice but to let her do whatever.

"Please change it back before we reach Tholituke…"

"Obviously. I'm sure Zenovia's heart would stop if she saw you blond." Ninym giggled, combing through his hair.

"Speaking of Zenovia. Do you think she knows?"

"Knows what?" Wein asked.

"—What else? The reason we're attending the ceremony."

"—To trade with Soljest, huh," Zenovia murmured.

Jiva nodded. "I believe that's why Prince Wein will be attending the ceremony."

They were in her office at the palace. Other vassals were in attendance, which was why she had on a more severe expression and tone than usual.

He continued with his explanation. "At this rate, it's only a matter of time before Marden becomes their strongest asset. By doing business with Soljest, which has access to maritime trade, I imagine they're looking for other ways to profit outside of this territory."

"I see... But if they're trying to close the economic gap between Natra and Marden... Doesn't that mean we'll be perceived as less of a threat?"

"Yes. That's right."

For the top brass of Marden, their highest priority was to stabilize their territory and assimilate into the bigger kingdom. With the wave of prosperity, they were basically calling attention to themselves, while Natra lagged behind. If Natra could secure another source of income, Marden would be able to integrate into the kingdom with no hard feelings.

This situation was a welcome one. There was no reason to interfere. Along with the vassals, Zenovia let out a sigh of relief.

Jiva continued. "By diminishing risk, we diminish our value. Look at us now. Marden is very valuable. Let's say we promise to slow our progress to support Natra. Maybe we can negotiate to get something from them, too."

Everyone began to stir.

"We just swore allegiance to them. Slowing our progress would only divide our people."

"Lady Zenovia is a member of the royal family. So what if we allied with Natra? Why should we dance to their tune?"

"Marden won't be able to uphold this prosperity on its own. We can't stop trading with the East."

As they discussed among themselves, Zenovia spoke up.

"To pull off this plan... We have one chance. We must settle this before he makes his way to Soljest. Right?"

"Indeed."

"In that case, we don't have much time to prepare... What do you think we should ask for in return, Jiva?"

He paused for a moment to think it over.

"—A marital union with Prince Wein, Lady Zenovia."

"So, do you plan on marrying Zenovia, Wein?"

"Nope," Wein said indifferently. "I imagine they'll try to bring it up. But I'm a man of my word: When push comes to shove, I'll abandon the kingdom eventually! ...Yow! Stop yanking my hair!"

"Sorry. My hand just slipped."

Very convenient, Wein thought to himself. Pointing it out would only invite her to pull his hair from the roots.

He sighed in resignation. "That aside, I want to stay single for the time being."

"And your ulterior motive?"

"To spend more time mingling with the ladies, obviously! I want to enjoy this for as long as possible! ...Stop! Ninym! I was just joking...! Put down the scissors! Stop trying to cut off my hair!"

"Sorry. Hand slipped again."

"I kid! I kid! The real reason is...I won't be able to dangle marriage as a negotiating tool to secure foreign alliances. That's why I have to be single!"

"Hmph...You have a point."

"Told you. Well, I guess I'll have to reconsider if our negotiations with Soljest fall through. I have two options: opening a new trade route or going the marriage route. Out of the two, I would want to avoid the latter, obviously. After all, I can reuse that one with other nations!"

Wein made it sound logical.

Ninym hesitated. "...Well, what about taking Zenovia as a mistress?"

"That'd be tough to pull off," he answered without missing a beat. "I mean, she used to be a princess. And I hear she's the glue holding the territory together. It would be one thing if I were already married, but if I asked her to be my mistress from the get-go, it would be like begging for Marden to fight against me."

If they tied the knot, the feudal lords would object that he was getting too comfortable with their newest territory. It would be hard to deal with resistance from the people of Marden on top of that.

"Basically, we just want to see if they will cooperate with us! If they're willing to lend us a hand, I imagine they'll push for our marital union. But my plan is to dodge the issue…!"

Huh. He sucks, Ninym thought.

"I imagine Prince Wein will try to avoid the subject of marriage," Jiva said.

All eyes were on him.

"At the very least, he will try to remain neutral until he can work things out with Soljest. Our course of action is to receive a solid answer during his stay."

"Then we won't be treated as outsiders anymore. It'd be easier to say our piece in the political realm," Zenovia observed.

"I imagine the other lords will not be pleased, but if Marden and the Arbalests combine forces, no one will be able to oppose it."

Jiva spoke the truth. The royal family and this territory were a cut above the rest. If their representatives tied the knot, they would be rock-solid.

"What do you think, Lady Zenovia? If I may have your approval, I shall begin preparations at once."

"……"

There was no reason to hesitate. Marrying Wein was the best thing for their future. It made sense to take advantage of their wealth to make their demands. After all, it would be mutually beneficial.

As a matter of politics, there was no reason to hold back.

So Zenovia gave her answer.

"By the way, Wein."

"Hmm? What's up?"

He didn't move a muscle as he looked at her.

Ninym seemed timid. "Um, well, this is a hypothetical situation, but…"

"…Uh-huh. Totally hypothetical. Gotcha. What?"

He never would have imagined seeing her this way.

Although his little sister liked to tack on this preface during their conversations, Wein was trying to figure out Ninym's reason for being cagey now.

"You won't get angry at me if I messed up your hair, right?"

"If you're asking me now, you already have, haven't you?"

Ninym averted his gaze. "Um… No? …Totally unrelated, but I think you should avoid mirrors for a while."

"W-wait. What?! What do you mean?! What did you do to my hair?!"

"I didn't think it would turn out this way…"

"Why do you look like you're giving up on me, Miss Ninym?!"

The carriage inched toward Tholituke as Wein writhed in agony—coming out of this situation as a loser once again.

"I appreciate you coming all this way, Prince Wein."

Wein's group had passed through the castle gates to Tholituke. Welcoming them into the renovated Elythro Palace was Zenovia, dressed to the nines in full regalia.

"You didn't need to come greet us at the door, Marquess of Marden."

She offered him a tiny smile. "No need to be so formal, Your Highness. 'Zenovia' is just fine."

"But you're a marquess and the former princess of Marden. I shouldn't be too casual, even if I am a prince."

"Nonsense. I've vowed vassalage to Natra. Not to mention, we've stood side by side on a battlefield. This isn't improper. It's a sign of our friendship."

"Hm..."

After making a show of thinking it over for a few moments, he smiled.

"Well then, I suppose I'll take you up on that, Lady Zenovia."

"We've prepared a modest celebration for you. Please follow me this way."

Led by Zenovia, they strode down the palace hallways.

"You did great things with the palace."

"Thank you. I must give credit to our subjects. They insisted we not leave our symbol burned to the ground."

"I caught a quick glimpse of the town on the way here. I was surprised to find hardly any trace of the war against Cavarin. I imagined the people of Marden would be in chaos, but I'm forever impressed by your skills, Lady Zenovia."

There was an underlying barb about her surprise attack to swear her vassalage...

"Only because Natra has welcomed us in. Had you not, the flag of Cavarin would be flying in these lands as we speak," she answered, breaking into an unexpected smile. "Our banquet is an expression of our gratitude... Hm?"

Her eyes traveled to his hair.

"Is something the matter?"

"It must be my imagination. I thought your hair seemed more brilliant than usual."

"...Ha-ha-ha. The sun of the golden age must have lightened it!"

Wein glanced behind him. Ninym avoided his gaze.

"Hee-hee. Is that it? A mischievous little sun."

"An outright insolent one, really..."

They had arrived at the reception hall.

Hmm, interesting.

One look told him everything he needed to know. The decor and cuisine were all from Natra.

It screams they want to be "one of us."

After all, they had intentionally shed their own culture to align themselves with Natra.

When the Imperial delegation had come to his kingdom, Wein had prepared their cuisine, too. However, Marden had taken it a step further by decking out their halls with new furnishings.

"I imagine you're tired from your journey. We wanted to prepare something familiar for you."

Wein and Zenovia sat in the seats of honor while his retinue was welcomed by the vassals of Marden. Ninym was standing at attention behind the prince, prepared for anything.

"Thank you for your consideration... Between the two of us, I'm relieved you prepared this. I think I can stop myself from slipping up in front of you, Zenovia."

"How kind of you, Your Highness."

He didn't just get a read of their concession. During the planning stages of the party, there had to be a fair share of vassals pushing to show their own culture, stubbornly holding on to their patriotism. However, the fact that Zenovia had reined in their opinions spoke to her skills.

I'm honestly impressed. Even though she's royalty, I imagine some people will look down on her as a woman.

Across the continent, there was a deep-seated belief that politics was a man's game.

In truth, many of the political leaders were men, which meant laws were made by men, for men, and upheld by men…a boys' club, so to speak.

If a woman tried to make room for herself, they would assume a look of mixed emotions. "Oh, um… That won't work…" they might stammer.

It had been the case when Zenovia earned a title of nobility in Natra.

As former foreign royalty, she possessed enough power to rival the Arbalests. It was only natural to bestow the title of marquess upon her.

However, it didn't stop the nobles from taking umbrage with this.

"Giving a woman the title of marquess is in poor judgment."

This was their basic argument, though they went through some mental gymnastics to make other excuses.

Though things varied by country, the nobility system was basically all make-believe—which was often symptomatic of these so-called "boys' clubs."

There were instances of women granted peerage in the history of Natra, but they were regarded as rare exceptions to the arbitrary rule that "noble rank is the privilege of men."

Well, I made it happen anyway.

They had tried to argue for a lower rank and the creation of a new female title, but one word from Wein was enough to make her a marquess, like he'd planned.

At any rate, it wasn't easy for a woman to stand on the political stage. Even so, Zenovia had captured the hearts of her people as the lord of Marden. It was honestly commendable.

"I hear the territory has become stable. I'm glad business is booming."

"Having viable industries is like a breath of fresh air." Zenovia nodded to herself. "I never imagined goods from the Empire would reap such profits."

"We're all attracted to things beyond reach."

"That seems to be the case. But I don't think that's the only explanation. We've been indoctrinated by the Teachings of Levetia that the East is comprised of barbaric groups who are ignorant to religion and capable of making only the crudest of items."

To devout followers, goods from the Empire were almost blasphemous. Despite their curiosity, many refused to have anything to do with them.

Then how did they develop a market for them?

"I was surprised. I never expected you to market them as products from Natra."

Wein purred. "It was a little scheme meant to ease the hearts of the pious and devout. I imagine they know the truth."

"You sound like a devil luring humans to hell."

"Oh, please. The devil is content with a mere human soul. It could never do business in gold like me."

They carried on in congenial conversation.

However, Wein didn't let down his guard for a moment, observing Zenovia.

This has been enough for me to understand her intentions.

All signs pointed to Marden wanting to cooperate with Natra, but that couldn't be everything up their sleeve. If Wein was on the mark, they would eventually bring up marriage.

But it would be boring for me to sit back and wait.

Wein waited for a lull in the conversation before pressing further.

"By the way, Lady Zenovia, it seems you're handling the affairs of Marden well. But rapid development could spell problems. If you have any concerns, I'd be happy to talk them over."

Fighting words. The vassals of Marden stirred.

"Let's see..."

However, Zenovia would not be moved. Not outwardly, at least. As Wein observed her closely, she seemed to think it over.

"You know, we've received a letter of protest from Delunio."

"Delunio? ...I see. So Marden got one, too?"

"Ah, I knew you received one as well."

Wein nodded. "What do you think of them, Lady Zenovia? We aren't on the best terms, so we don't have much information on them."

"Yes, well..." Zenovia thought for a moment. "I know their citizens have long been followers of Levetia. They hold their culture in high esteem. They're known for being a conservative nation. A young king has recently taken the throne, but the prime minister, Sirgis, is handling most political matters."

Zenovia continued. "Sirgis is very patriotic and a devout follower of Levetia. Since being granted real authority, he's made it his mission to protect their culture and spread the teachings."

"Sounds like a tough place to live."

"Yes. To preserve their own ideologies, he's been critical of other nations. The youth aren't his biggest fans, and even the conservatives think he's going too far. It seems his politics have played a part in their deteriorating relationship with Soljest."

Got it, Wein thought.

Soljest traded with other nations, which resulted in the spread of goods and ideas. It must have annoyed someone like Sirgis, who seemed to be a cultural purist.

"In that context, the letter makes sense. Soljest isn't the only one committing this 'offense.' Marden is importing goods and customs through the Empire."

"It was just a letter this time, but I imagine they'll send a diplomat before resorting to military force. The correspondence included a request for a meeting. I declined because it coincided with Your Highness's visit." Zenovia looked at him for help.

Wein grinned. "Ignore it and keep doing business."

"Are you sure?"

"If they only sent a letter, they can't be *that* upset. Start taking them seriously when there's a line of messengers protesting at your door."

"I see. Then that's how I'll proceed."

Wein gave a satisfied nod before realizing something.

...Hm? The conversation is over.

When he asked if she had any concerns, he thought she'd allude to the domestic disparity or a martial union—but it seemed he was off the mark.

I guess she can't stand the idea of dancing to my tune. Does that mean she's about to make her move?

Wein stayed on guard as he continued talking to Zenovia.

Hm?

Neither she nor her vassals broached the subject of marriage.

What?!

As their conversation went on, he grew more confused—

Huuuuh——?!

Finally, the banquet came to an end...

...All without Zenovia uttering one word about marriage.

"...That was weird."

Wein had returned to the room prepared for him. He crossed his arms.

"Even though I tried to bait her, she never mentioned marriage..."

"I was surprised myself." Ninym had been watching their exchange. "It seems to me like she actually may have been actively trying to avoid it."

"But there's no better time to bring up this proposal..." Wein groaned. "Nghhh."

Next to him, Ninym offered a small smile. "And you were so confident when you said they would demand marriage."

"Ack."

"Yet instead of acting the way you hoped, they completely avoided the topic."

"Ngh."

"Could this be what they call 'an inflated ego'?"

"AAAAAAAH?!"

The barrage of verbal knives brought Wein to his knees.

"Th-this can't be happening... I was supposed to suavely turn down her proposal..."

"By the end of the banquet, it was like you were begging for one. It was honestly pathetic."

"GAAAAAAAAH?!" He collapsed onto the floor.

Someone knocked on the door.

"I do *not* have an ego..." Wein glared at Ninym as she went to answer it.

Outside the room stood Jiva, who served Zenovia.

"I apologize for interrupting you at this hour. I would like to briefly discuss your schedule for tomorrow."

Ninym quickly looked behind her. Just a moment prior, Wein

had been a dead man on the floor, but he'd managed to sit straight in a chair, holding a book in one hand and looking perfectly regal.

"I don't mind. Show him in, Ninym."

"Right this way, Sir Jiva."

Jiva entered the room as he was bidden.

Wein looked at him. "How can I help you?"

"I'm terribly sorry for visiting at this hour. You were scheduled for a meeting over lunch with Lady Zenovia, but something came up that requires her attention. I came to inform you she may not have the time."

Wein and Ninym exchanged a look.

A sudden change in schedule wasn't strange. Wein knew the feeling himself.

However, his stay was their chance to put their plans into action. After all, Wein was on his way to Soljest, departing Marden in two or three days. It made more sense to leave any governmental affairs on hold until afterward.

It must be a huge deal if she's postponing our lunch meeting—

It didn't take him long to cancel out that possibility. Despite calling it an "emergency," Jiva didn't seem to be especially frazzled.

In that case, she might be trying to distance herself from me. Then why would she throw a fancy welcome party? I got the impression she wanted to work together.

Her moves weren't adding up. Wein thought of a number of hypotheses, but none held any weight or connected any dots.

Thinking wasn't getting him anywhere. Wein spoke up.

"In that case, I guess there isn't much we can do. It's unfortunate that things didn't work out, but the stability of Marden is crucial to Natra. Please tell Lady Zenovia that I gave her the go-ahead to take care of her official duties."

"I will. Thank you for your understanding, Your Highness." Jiva bowed.

Ninym spoke up beside him. "That means our schedule will be empty in the afternoon."

"You're right. There are plenty of ways to kill time, but..." Wein mused.

Jiva raised his head. "About that. I would love to guide you around the city."

"Oh. The city, huh?"

He nodded. "When we were first liberated, our streets were ravaged by war, and I believe I remember things kept you busy from seeing our town for what it is, Your Highness. I would be delighted for you to observe our efforts to revitalize the territory."

"Hmm..."

Obviously, this wasn't going to be some stroll through town. Wein could tell the man was up to something—but it was hard to say what exactly.

Well, guess we've got no choice but to just go along with it.

Wein nodded. "Sounds good to me. I'm looking forward doing some sightseeing tomorrow. Ninym, I'll leave the details up to you."

"Understood."

"Thank you very much. I'll prepare a guide." Jiva bowed again. "Well, I'll take my leave. I'm grateful for your willingness to speak with me."

He turned on his heel and quietly exited the room.

Ninym tilted her head, looking troubled. "I wonder what that was all about."

"No idea, but something is bound to happen tomorrow. I'll finally find out why there's been no talk of marriage yet...I think!"

"I hope it's not just your ego talking. For your sake."

"Anything but that...! My pride is on the line here...!"

Wein secretly prayed as he awaited the coming day.

The following afternoon.

"I apologize for the wait, Prince Wein."

The guide before them was a former member of the retinue that had accompanied them to the Cavarin capital. She had disguised herself as a young man.

Zeno.

Ah, I get it now... Wein concluded.

I see, Ninym thought.

They immediately understood the situation.

Zeno was Zenovia in disguise. She'd had reason to hide her identity before, but Wein was taken aback by her reappearance.

"I'm honored to meet you again, Your Highness."

"Uh-huh. Sure... By the way, Zeno, what are you up to now?"

"I'm one of Lady Zenovia's attendants. Since she's so busy, I keep an eye on the city in her place."

That was the pretend scenario. As "Zeno," Zenovia could take a little break from her official duties. Wein didn't do that for safety reasons, but he could understand the feeling of wanting to get away and walk around town once in a while.

"I have a message from Lady Zenovia."

Zeno cleared her throat.

"'Please think of your guide as me and enjoy seeing the sights. Feel free to ask any questions. Walking through town is a good chance for conversation.'"

"...I see."

Instead of a typical meeting, she planned to have an open discussion as they strolled through the city. She must have had some things she couldn't say as a feudal lord to a regent.

©Falmaro

Wein gave a wry smile and finally nodded. "Well then, I'll take Lady Zenovia up on that offer. Lead the way, Zeno."

"Understood. Right this way."

With Zeno guiding them, Wein stepped into the city proper.

"This is the central plaza."

Zeno led them straight ahead into the heart of the city.

"When thinking about Tholituke, the first thing that comes to mind is its bronze statues."

Statues of horsemen circled the outer rim of the plaza. A bronze king on horseback stood at the very center.

"This is the first ruler of Marden. The others depict his most trusted men."

"Hmm… I don't recall seeing this when you were liberated."

"Cavarin took it away during the occupation…" Zeno replied with frustration before straightening her spine. "However, it was safely returned via negotiation. It's a part of our history, so the vassals were all relieved."

"That's fortunate. You'll have to make sure it never happens again."

"You're right. I hope to prevent anyone from ever melting them."

Metals were an indispensable part of warfare, so there were never enough. With a shortage of weapons, statues were often broken down and repurposed.

"Marden has not fully recovered from battle. Our hearts may have calmed, but another war will send us spiraling. I wish peace were here to stay."

"I totally agree, but I don't think you need to be so worried," Wein said, testing the waters. "If this boom lasts, Marden will be a powerhouse. Once you reach that status, you'll be able to push aside any outside forces that get in your way."

"Strength is crucial. But in excess, it can lead to problems. For now, I believe it is more important for us to be accepted as a part of Natra."

"I wonder about that."

He seemed to probe her with his eyes, searching for the truth.

"Won't it be better if you became more powerful, joined forces with another nation, and strived for independence?"

Zeno laughed. "You love to joke around. Based on your accomplishments, it would be foolish for us to band with another nation and cross swords with Natra. It's like jumping into the sea with an anchor tied to your foot."

"Huh... I wonder if Lady Zenovia feels the same way."

"Of course," Zeno replied assuredly. "Even the vassals believe that future prosperity lies in being accepted as part of your kingdom."

"I see..."

Their smiles seemed combative. Their gazes seemed to examine each other.

For a few beats, they seemed determined to get the truth out of their opponent—even if it was the tiniest fragment.

Zeno was the first to break away.

"Let's head to the next location. There is so much to see."

They continued their stroll through Tholituke. Zeno guided them to the carved fountain, a time-worn bridge that spanned across the river, and everything else the city had to offer. He could tell from the joy in her voice that she wasn't just knowledgeable about this place; she loved it.

"...Phew. That took some time."

They had covered most of the town. The party was taking a break at a restaurant Zeno often frequented. She'd apparently rented out the entire establishment ahead of time.

"What is your honest opinion of Tholituke?"

"I gotta say, I'm impressed," Wein replied, holding a cup of black tea. "The tourist spots were incredible, but I think I was most moved by your people. It's clear they have faith in Lady Zenovia."

"We have high hopes for her, especially with this new economic boom."

"That's good to hear. There's nothing bad about building trust between politicians and the people. Of course, you can't be too careful."

Wein hadn't thought twice about that statement, but Zeno seemed to latch on to it.

"I've been meaning to ask… What makes you so wary of the people, Your Highness?"

"What?" Wein blinked back.

He wondered if she might be trying to get something out of him, but her behavior seemed to indicate otherwise.

Zeno hemmed and hawed. "I guess that's the wrong word… Maybe 'distant'? There's something weird about your relationship with them… I guess it just struck me when you said before I should view the people as mere accomplices in achieving my own goals."

"Oh right." Wein smiled at the memory. "I did say that, but… that's strange. I remember talking to Lady Zenovia."

"Ah. Oh…um…I heard it from her." Her cheeks flushed with embarrassment.

Wein laughed dryly as the gears in his mind began to turn. "About that… I have a question for you, Zeno. Do you think royal blood is precious?"

"What?"

Her eyes widened, but she didn't miss a beat.

"Yes… Of course. As representatives of the people and rulers of the land, nobility and royalty are to be treasured. It isn't just the aristocrats who think that way. Commoners do, too."

Wein nodded. She wasn't wrong: This concept of lineage was nothing new. It was a system of values held by almost everyone.

"Well then, here's another question: When did it become important?"

"…When?"

This time, Zeno had to stop and think. She must not have ever reflected on it. Her face grew troubled as if she were looking at a numeric formula. Wein decided to extend a helping hand.

"I'm a member of the royal family in Natra. If you think noble lineage means something, that suggests mine does, too. In that case, when did my blood gain value?"

Zeno thought for a few moments. "…You've always had it. Your blood has possessed worth since you were born as King Owen's son."

"That's right. A child born into royalty inherits royal blood. If that's true, when did Owen become someone of importance?"

"Since King Owen's father was royalty… When he was born?"

"Exactly. Children born into royalty have worth because their parents have value. And their parents, because of their parents' parents. Logic, really. Simple." Wein looked over at Ninym. "If we trace back my lineage, where will we end up?"

"One of the founder of Levetia's lead disciples, Caleus."

One of Wein's ancestors was King Salema, who founded Natra and once was the prince of a country known as Naliavene. That meant Wein's lineage dated back to its history, all the way to Caleus.

"The great disciple. Ask anyone about his blood. You'd be hard pressed to find someone who thinks it doesn't have value. Until Levetia discovered Caleus, he had been nothing more than a worthless peasant, which means his parents were peasants, too. Let me ask you again. When did Caleus's blood become valuable?"

"That was..."

If the parents were important, so was their child. However, Caleus wasn't born with noble blood. In other words, there had been a point in his life when it had crossed this boundary...

"...When he began to follow Levetia and found great success."

"That's right," Wein replied. "Was it raw power, intelligence, eloquence, or just plain old luck? Any one of his strengths could have been the catalyst. But a nameless man had managed to achieve something and make a name for himself... And that's how his blood and his descendants were seen as valuable. Trace back the history of any 'precious' lineage today, and this is where you'll start."

"...I think I understand. But what does that have to do with my question?"

"Don't you get it? We're drunk on our power, but go back a few centuries, and you'll find we were once commoners. That means commoners today have the potential to become nobility and royalty one day."

"——Ngh!"

Zeno looked like she couldn't believe it.

It made sense when he put it like that. She'd just never realized it before. Or maybe she was playing willful ignorance. It was hard to blame her. How could she go against her own position as royalty?

But the prince is right... I can't believe he can admit that himself...

It wasn't just a scathing critique of the monarchy. It was a statement that could totally flip what it meant to be noble. If anyone else had said this out loud, they would have been hauled off to the guillotines—yet the tone of this future king made it seem like he was discussing the weather.

"Back to your original question... Why am I wary toward my people? The population of Natra is close to five hundred thousand people. Well, I guess we're closer to eight hundred thousand with

Marden. There's got to be more than a handful of nameless candidates watching my every move throughout my entire reign… Why wouldn't I be looking over my shoulder?"

A shiver went down Zeno's spine. She'd never thought of commoners in that light. However, she could now see why he believed it was stranger to be blindly trusting.

Wein wasn't pooh-poohing his subjects. He knew he had to fulfill his people's needs. Otherwise, things would take a sour turn, and the nameless would drive him out. Just as his own ancestors had.

I finally get it… He doesn't think his lineage is anything special.

Zeno finally realized why Wein had said they should think of the people as accomplices—a means to an end.

It wasn't any different from a child of a baker encouraged to take over the family business by their environment, propelled by a demand for bread. Wein had been born into royalty, pushed to become a monarch over a nation because the people needed him. That was all there was to it.

If the people decided he no longer served a purpose, he would step down from the throne with a little chuckle.

How ironic that Wein understood his people more than she did, even though she'd bragged about leading the masses and he'd admitted to seeing his subjects as mere accomplices.

"That's why royalty like to mythologize themselves. If they can get people to believe that they came from gods, their authority is harder to shake. In the case of Natra, Caleus has become lionized nowadays, so… What's wrong, Zeno?"

"It's nothing…" She offered him a smile as he looked at her quizzically. "I'm just in awe of your capacity as prince. Pay me no mind."

"Really?" He blinked back before shrugging his shoulders. "Thanks, but I haven't been too confident about that lately."

"Why not? There isn't anyone with more fame than you."

"That's what I thought." Wein went in for the kill. "To tell you the truth, I thought someone was going to propose to me. But now I've been wondering if it's all in my head."

"……"

It took no time for Zenovia to realize he was talking about her.

"Maybe she's already gotten betrothed behind my back?"

It was in Marden's best interests for Zenovia to marry Wein. However, that wasn't to say there weren't other suitors. There had been a fair share of powerful nations trying to get on good terms with Marden. If she had already promised her hand in marriage to someone else, it would spark new problems with Natra, meaning it was better for Marden to keep this under wraps.

"…I know of no suitors…" Zeno chose her words carefully. "I don't think she has time to think about marriage, especially when she has her hands full with things requiring her immediate attention as a citizen of Marden."

"…But can't she settle those 'things' by marrying me?"

"Maybe, but—"

Zeno stopped herself. After a few seconds of silence, she laughed at him in a mocking way.

"There might be a more simple reason to explain this."

"What could that be?"

"Perhaps she can't stand your face!"

"……" Wein hung his head.

"Um, that was a joke. Please don't look so sad."

"……"

"U-um. Well, this has been lovely, but I think it's about time we returned to the palace!"

"……"

"A-at this time of day, the city looks totally different! Why don't we take the long way home?"

As Zeno tried her best to keep the vibe light, they started to trudge back to the palace.

"*...Phew.*"

Having parted from Wein and taken off her disguise, Zenovia let out a sigh in her office.

"Excellent work today, Lady Zenovia," Jiva praised.

"Any issues during my absence?"

"None whatsoever," he declared. "Some paperwork needs to be looked over... But we can handle that after we see them off tomorrow."

Zenovia nodded. "It hasn't been easy, but it looks like we'll make it through somehow."

"Yes. All thanks to you... It seems he actually asked about a marital union today on your expedition."

"He seemed to wonder what was taking so long." She averted her eyes. "...I'm sorry, Jiva, for ignoring your advice to marry him."

"Are you hearing yourself? You're the ruler of this territory, Lady Zenovia. You will always be our top priority," he replied. "Besides, I understand your feelings. Prince Wein is..."

"Uh-huh," Zenovia confirmed with a humorless smile. "I could never tell him, but...he's aloof and a little frightening."

Her feelings for Wein were complicated.

Her biggest one was gratitude to him for aiding the Liberation Army. The next one was empathy and respect as a young leader, followed by envy and a feeling of inferiority over his accomplishments. She feared his frame of mind and ideas, which almost seemed divorced from his royal position, yet admired his craftiness and grit.

In summary, Wein was a distant, incredible, scary brand of hero.

"From our tour today and past interactions, I'm painfully aware I could never be his wife."

If Zenovia were to marry Wein, she would naturally become his princess consort.

Back when she had known nothing about him, she would have been all in. However, though their time together had been short, Zenovia had come to view him in a hero's light. She did not have confidence she could be the wind beneath his wings.

"Besides, his princess consort is the future queen. And that comes with many duties..."

She had been raised sheltered. Though she was studying up a storm, she was sorely lacking, which came at the cost of burdening her vassals. Handling the territory was tough enough. If she became Wein's wife, she'd be weighed down with responsibility for Natra as a whole.

If there was peace, she could have rested in the palace in Natra, far from politics.

Not only was this was a period of unrest, but Natra was trying to make huge strides. If Zenovia became queen, her appointed role would not be a small one. She just didn't believe in herself.

She'd already gotten a peek into Pandora's box. Her decision was a simple one.

She knew marrying Wein would be a brilliant move, but her heart just wasn't in it.

"I'm a failure..."

It would be much, *much* better if Imperial Princess Lowellmina married Wein. In fact, Zenovia would have taken the plunge if that were the case, serving as his mistress with the permission of her eager vassals. In fact, she had considered asking him about Princess Lowellmina during the welcome party.

Jiva suddenly spoke up. "Excuse me for overstepping boundaries, but when we wrestled this city from Cavarin's grip, the vassals made two vows to you, Lady Zenovia."

"What vows?" she asked, tilting her head.

Jiva continued. "One: We would do everything for the good of Marden. Two: We would never force you down a path against your will, even if it was the best thing for the territory."

Zenovia's eyes widened. She had known her vassals were giving it their best effort, but she never imagined they would go that far.

"If you feel that marriage to Prince Wein is not the answer, that's all right. We're coming together to form the best plan yet. Please be at ease." He offered a small smile. "Between the two of us, I proposed this out of my duty as your vassal. Personally, I wasn't too keen on this union."

"Don't you think highly of Prince Wein?"

"Of course. I don't even have the right to appraise him. But his personality and conduct give cause for alarm… When I heard he'd slain the king of Cavarin and set fire to the city to make his escape, it made me doubt his sanity, to say the very least."

"Ah. Well, that was rather off-putting to me as well."

"Instead of agonizing over what's past, it's crucial that we face forward," he'd said during the fiasco, which grossed her out even more. Anyone with an ounce of common sense could see why no sane woman would choose to be his wife.

"You will need to get married at some point to secure an heir, but there are more than enough suitors for you. With successful negotiations between Natra and Soljest, we won't be in any more danger, and you will have time to consider it at your leisure. We can discuss it with everyone."

"You're right… Thank you, Jiva."

"Not at all. This is part of my duties." He gave the young leader a reverent bow.

"Pardon me...!" A flustered official flew into the office.

"What is it?! Did something happen?" Jiva asked.

"Just now, at the main gate of the palace—"

Zenovia's and Jiva's eyes grew wide at the report.

Meanwhile, Wein was back in his room.

"An ugly man with a huge ego, huh..." he groaned as he stretched across the middle of the bed.

"Can you please get over it? It was her last-ditch excuse."

Ninym was next to him. Nothing seemed to improve his mood.

She sighed. "Seems Zenovia has no plans to secretly team up with some other nation. That's vital insight."

"But now I really don't know why she didn't propose!"

"Maybe...some personal circumstances?"

"Like what?"

"...Like you're not her type?"

"Be right back! Gonna kill myself!"

"Jump out from the window, and you're just going to break your legs...!"

Wrestling Wein away from the window, Ninym searched for the right words to say.

"Besides, you can still be hot and not her type."

"Say it. Tell me I'm hot."

"...Do you hear something?"

"Hey! Don't try to make excuses...! How typical, Miss Ninym...!"

"No. Wait." She ignored his wailing.

He realized she was right when she opened the door. They could hear something happening outside.

"Wait here, Wein. I'm going to check."

"While you're gone, I'm going to sulk and hibernate forever."

"It's barely autumn." She flashed him a dry smile before leaving the room.

It wasn't long before she returned with a panicked look on her face.

"This is bad, Wein. It looks like Marden has a surprise guest."

"Who could that be?" He cocked his head to the side.

Ninym was all serious. "The prime minister of Delunio, Sirgis."

—*How did this happen?*

Zenovia's mind turned this over in one of the palace's reception rooms.

A short man sat directly across from her. His name was Sirgis, born a commoner, now serving as the prime minister of Delunio.

"I apologize for imposing on you with no warning, Princess Zenovia… I mean, Marquess," Sirgis corrected pointedly as he bowed his head.

Nothing was warm about her gaze. "For a prime minister to breach the rules of conduct… You must know this reflects poorly on your kingdom."

Her unapproachable attitude made Sirgis stiffen, as well as her aide Jiva and her guard Borgen.

"Jiva, she seems pissed," Borgen whispered.

He gave the tiniest nod. "It's not just about bad manners. Prince Wein is staying with us. She doesn't want anyone to steal her fun."

"But isn't she being too difficult?"

"That's just how it is." Jiva sighed. "After all, Lady Zenovia hates Delunio."

"What?" Borgen's eyebrows shot up.

Sirgis replied. "I understand your anger. However, I'm only here to resolve a pressing issue between Delunio and Marden. I ask for your understanding."

"What issue? That doesn't ring any bells."

"Oh please." Sirgis seemed unfazed. "You must have received our letter. We have concerns regarding your exported goods." His tone made it clear he wouldn't allow any excuses.

Zenovia put on a superficial smile as she thought it over.

—*You're going down, Prime Piece of Shit.*

Back when Marden was its own kingdom, they had been on relatively good terms with Soljest and Delunio. At least, from their perspective.

However, Cavarin took over their capital in the previous year. Zenovia had tried to lead her remaining forces in a revolt against their control, but they had found themselves at a disadvantage. She had to ask the two nations for their assistance.

Those hopes were in vain, as no reply came from either nation. King Gruyere of Soljest thought nothing of Marden, and Sirgis wanted to avoid making an enemy of Cavarin since they hosted the Holy Elites.

In the end, Marden joined with Natra and took back the capital, but it did nothing to alleviate the feeling of betrayal experienced by Zenovia and her vassals.

"Based on her ladies-in-waiting..." Jiva whispered. "As a young girl, Zenovia used to have a little puppy, which wandered into the palace gardens one day. There, it died from a snake bite."

"And?"

"Lady Zenovia became despondent. After its burial, she spent four days looking for the snake. Apparently, she killed it with her own sword."

"......"

"She loves Marden with all her heart. However, her emotions have another side to them."

In other words, Cavarin, Soljest, Delunio, and even Levetia were on her hit list. Zenovia was pissed that a representative of Delunio had popped in unannounced to complain about trading.

"Even if you say you have concerns..." Zenovia began. "We have done nothing wrong. If you've come with false allegations, I must ask you to leave."

"I take it you have no interest in discussion?"

"Is this how you handle discussions in your country? By barging in and trying to shove your opinions down my throat? Seems to be a cultural difference, if you ask me."

"...It's sad to see you're taking your demotion so hard."

They shot daggers at each other. Gone was any pretense of civility. Those listening could do nothing more than watch in trepidation.

"I guess there's no way around it. I have no choice but to speak directly with the royal family of Natra."

"Oh yeah? Well, don't expect me to cooperate."

"Is that so?" Sirgis replied. "Isn't the prince here? I wish to meet him."

"......"

Zenovia finally understood.

Sirgis had banked on this. By showing up uninvited during Wein's stay, he could speak to her senior if she refused to cooperate. It made total sense, really.

This was the first time someone had treated her with such disrespect.

I'm gonna murder him.

She felt like she might fly into a killer rage.

I must remain calm. As Prince Wein once said, it's barbaric to take out one's sword in the middle of a meeting.

This was the political realm. She couldn't act rashly. Zenovia remembered what Wein had taught her and steadied her heart.

—Well, Wein *had* assassinated King Ordalasse of Cavarin.

But I have to stop Sirgis right now…

Allowing him to meet Wein wasn't an option. However, her opponent wasn't going to back off easily.

The door to the room opened as she tried to figure out an exit strategy.

"No need to worry, Lady Zenovia," assured a young man—Wein.

He grinned. "If you wish to speak with me, I'm all ears, Prime Minister."

"It's a pleasure to meet you. I'm Wein, the crown prince of Natra."

"Sirgis. Prime minister of Delunio. I've heard things about you, Your Highness."

Wein sat down as they exchanged greetings.

"Your Highness," Zenovia whispered in his ear. "Are you sure about this?"

"Leave it to me," he whispered in return before turning back to Sirgis. "I'm happy to talk, but I've got a full schedule. I hate to rush you, but let's make this quick. It's about exported items, right?"

"Precisely." Sirgis nodded. "The goods from the Empire travel via Natra… We would like for you to cease this activity."

His request came as no surprise. Delunio was conservative with a fair number of pious followers. The encroaching goods were basically an eyesore.

"The Empire is power-hungry. You know they aren't satisfied with just ravishing the East. They're trying to advance into the West as well. The Teachings of Levetia seek peace on the continent and the salvation of its people. One could say the Empire is a bitter enemy. If their goods spread across the West, we'll basically be allowing their vanguard onto our doorstep. I understand your kingdom has ties to the East, but with Marden serving as your vassal nation, we wish you would act in alignment with the West."

There was something about his speech that was dignified and intelligent. His rise from commoner to prime minister seemed to be founded on skill. However, Wein was ready for his request, which meant he'd already concocted a way to take him down.

"Yes, I understand where you're coming from," Wein replied, with a hint of a smile. "However, there seems to be a misunderstanding, Sir Sirgis. While we have been more involved in trade lately, these goods are made in Natra."

This was their official stance. Selling under their name didn't just make it easier for the devout to make purchases. It served as a convenient excuse when dealing with foreign nations.

"That's how you intend to get out of this?"

"Ouch. You're more than welcome to look at the goods on the market. See for yourself that they're made in our kingdom."

Sirgis seemed disgusted. "...*Some* of them are made in Natra. I admit we were shell-shocked when we unraveled your scheme: distributing goods from the Empire as yours. As demand increases, you've been selling authentic products from Natra, posing as ones from the West. Very clever, indeed."

It was difficult to develop an eye for things, especially for goods from another part of the world. They didn't have the experience to judge whether something was fake or real, good or bad.

However, it was human nature to want to dip into fads. With the popularity of any item, unsavory types took advantage of the moment to sell their inferior wares.

Wein had been at the forefront of this scheme.

"Like the clothes from the Empire..." the prime minister continued. "I thought the colors were too bold, like that bright yellow. You must have planned to create something flashy to draw the eye. Plus, by making the buyer focus on color, no one would notice if the rest of the garment was thrown together sloppily. Even if they had their doubts, peer pressure would do them in... An impressive scam," Sirgis spat.

"I have no idea what you're talking about. It isn't strange for there to be differences in quality." Wein shrugged his shoulders. "Think about it. According to Levetia, the East is full of savages, right? Do you honestly think they could create items to suit our refined taste?"

"Th-that's..."

It was a scathing counter. Even Sirgis was aware of the reality of life in the East. However, admitting the truth would mean facing their lack of advancement and denying the teachings. It was a difficult question for any pious believer to answer.

Still, Sirgis was the prime minister of an entire nation. He went at it from a different angle.

"Even if that's the case, the West has upheld a general rule since the enactment of the Circulous Law to avoid excessive interference, such as collecting tolls from pilgrims and forcing them to purchase goods! Don't you realize you're in violation of this rule?"

The Circulous Law had been officially put into effect one hundred years prior—with the intent to cut out the East from the pilgrimage. The heads of Levetia needed to offer a few incentives to get the believers to accept it. This gave special privileges to pilgrims such as tax exemptions and protection from bandits and pushy merchants.

"As you said, Sir Sirgis, that is the general rule. It would be one thing if it were officially sanctioned by Levetia, but it has no legal power."

If declared a legal ordinance, someone might abuse the system. One hundred years prior, each nation left enough wiggle room to act around the rule as necessary. It was understood to be an unspoken benefit for Western nations.

Wein had ripped that secret knowledge to shreds.

If this was a meeting where everyone was congenial…

"Let's be nice to the pilgrims."

"Sure."

"Yeah, that sounds good."

…He was basically an invasive species, jeopardizing the ecosystem.

"Hey, easy pickings! Be right back! Gonna ravish this land!"

That was his MO.

"As a royal, you must understand the importance of this hundred-year custom. Disrespecting it is the same as throwing mud in the face of Levetia…!"

"Hmm."

The Teachings of Levetia were deeply rooted in the West. Even Wein didn't want to stir up trouble with them.

Sirgis had switched up his argument.

"If you're saying my policies are harmful to Levetia, that's fine," Wein said. "But why haven't I heard directly from them?"

"……Ngh!" Sirgis's face twisted.

"You're just a believer—not even a Holy Elite. I don't think you have the right to speak for them."

Wein knew this scheme would rub Levetia the wrong way. It wouldn't be surprising at all if they sent their own cease and desist.

I'll just rack up the cash until that happens.

How long could he hold out until Levetia put in real effort to stop him? Delunio had no place in this conversation.

"Well, Sir Sirgis? Do you have anything else to say?"

"……"

Wein was never going to admit the goods were from the Empire. Sirgis didn't have the right to speak for Levetia.

It was obvious from his pained expression that the prime minister had nothing. He hung his head.

"Why did it have to be them instead of me...?!" he muttered through gnashed teeth.

Wein didn't catch a single word, but he could feel his rage.

Can you...? Wein motioned for the guards to step in, thinking of the worst-case scenario.

They must have already sensed Sirgis's mental state. They were ready for battle.

The moment seemed to stretch for eternity...until Sirgis relaxed all the tension in his shoulders.

"...It seems we cannot reach an understanding." Sirgis stood up swiftly. His expression was cold. "I suppose there's no way. I will discuss the matter with my homeland and go from there."

"I see. It's unfortunate, but I'm sure there will be other opportunities."

"I hope you're right... Well then, I bid you farewell." Sirgis turned on his heel, his attendants hurriedly following behind.

Just as he was about to leave, he looked back.

"Allow me to say one last thing."

He took a breath.

"You will regret this someday."

Wein answered this curse with a grin. "I'll pray to God that day never comes."

Spearheading his group as they quickly left the palace, Sirgis meditated inside the carriage. His mind turned over the conversation with the prince of Natra.

"I didn't expect him to be so shameless," barked an angry passenger, a subordinate.

His aides' irritation was to be expected, considering their prime minister's main argument had been completely dismissed.

Sirgis was calm in comparison.

"It would have saved us trouble if everything had worked out. But we knew it wouldn't work out that way. We received word en route that the prince was staying in Marden, and we decided to investigate. It's enough to know more about his personality," Sirgis continued. "More importantly, our main prize is at our next destination."

"Do you think it will go well?"

"The plan is already in motion. It has to go well if we wish for Delunio to become its most ideal form."

His carriage raced down the road.

"It pains me to part ways. Thank you for your hospitality, Lady Zenovia."

It had been a day since Wein managed to strong-arm Sirgis in place.

His party was ready to set off on schedule.

"I'm sorry you had to sit through that affair yesterday, Your Highness."

"Don't mention it. We made it through. Plus, it was nice to get to know Sir Sirgis. Besides," Wein continued, "I don't think we've seen the last of Delunio. There's a good chance they're up to something. Don't let your guard down."

"I won't… Well then, take care, Prince Wein." She bowed.

Wein nodded as he set off for Soljest with his retinue.

"...*Hff.*"

Having seen them off, Zenovia let out a sigh of relief. Her vassals followed suit.

"We can finally relieve some of the tension," Jiva said.

Zenovia nodded, though her profile remained stoic. "We must catch up on government matters that need our attention."

"We will take care of them. Rest easy, Lady Zenovia..."

"I wasn't raised to sleep soundly while others are hard at work."

If Wein were here, he would have offered to nap extra hard.

To Jiva, Zenovia's words were law.

"As you wish. But please do not overexert yourself."

"Understood. Let us get to work."

It seemed Marden would return to a state of normalcy.

However, not even a week after Wein's departure, a single letter addressed to Zenovia turned their territory upside down.

Phithcha was known as a sprawling harbor town and the capital of Soljest. It served as the foundation and prided symbol of the nation.

Blessed with good trade, it hadn't always been the capital city. However, once Gruyere had taken over the throne, he relocated it and expanded the port.

Phithcha became the capital both in name and substance.

"I'd heard the stories, but they give Mealtars a run for its money."

A few days had passed since they left the capital of Marden, Tholituke. Inside the carriage, Wein expressed his admiration as they traveled down the main drag of Phithcha.

"Even though we're both in the North, the port seems to make a world of difference."

Ninym couldn't hide her amazement either.

Natra had no warm-water port. At the northernmost tip of the continent, their oceans were frozen solid for over half the year. This was a death sentence in both military and economic pursuits. They could sail for only six months out of the year, and the cost of maintaining their warships only continued to mount. In Wein's opinion, they were about as useless as scrap paper, and he wished he could chuck them in a wastebasket. *"He shoots, he scooores!"* Wein imagined calling out.

Any shipmaster who stopped at this dead end would wonder what he did to deserve this punishment.

"Functional ports are nice... Do you think they'll switch with us? Well, I guess you can't technically call our fishing village a 'port'..."

"I mean, no one is eager to set up shop in a place that's only functional half the time..."

"And we can't change anything about the weather... Oh, what are they selling at that food stall? I've never seen anything like it."

"I heard the ceremony is a time to enjoy culinary offerings of the continent. Based on what I'm seeing, I don't think they were exaggerating. I suppose their self-proclaimed title as the capital of the culinary world holds up."

"I'd say. Besides, this place has brine in the air, docked boats, and rows of fresh fish... Though they're both doing well for themselves, Mealtars is inland. This has a different vibe." Wein clutched his stomach. "...I gotta admit, this is making me hungry."

"We're almost to our destination. I'm sure they'll have plenty for us to eat."

"I hope it's enough to satisfy my empty stomach."

Their discussion carried on as the carriage made its way to the palace.

To get straight to the point, the palace was enormous.

These royal edifices were known for being large. They served to display one's authority and function as places of administration. It required an appropriate amount of space to accommodate heavy foot traffic.

But this...was on another level. Compared to the downsized palace in Marden and their humble abode in Natra, it was almost astronomical in size.

"...It seems almost *too* big to be functional. I think they might have gone overboard," Ninym commented from within the carriage as it came to a halt in front of the palace.

Wein did not chime in to agree with her.

"Oh right," he remembered. "You've never seen King Gruyere."

"Hm? Yeah. As a Flahm, I can't imagine any good would come out of meeting him."

"Well, now's your chance. You can come along with me. You'll see why this place is so huge."

"...Consider this your warning: Don't do anything stupid. Okay?"

"*Pssh.* Don't worry. I promise to think through my actions when the time comes."

This did nothing to ease her concerns, but this was her master's order. She was curious to find out more about the rumored king. The original plan would have left her behind in Natra, but she ended up concealing herself as one of his attendants.

"We've been expecting you, Prince Wein."

As they alighted from the carriage, a row of officials bowed to them.

"We'll guide you to the audience hall as His Majesty has requested. Right this way."

Wein nodded and began to follow behind the officials. Ninym blended in with the rest of the attendants, following after him...

Hm? That's...

In a corner of the palace grounds was a carriage parked far away. She couldn't be sure because of the distance, but she had a feeling she'd seen it a few days prior—

Ack! Don't leave without me!

Ninym hurried to catch up with the rest of the crowd.

They stepped into the palace, promptly greeted by a spacious interior. The walls were lined with statues and sculptures. However, there were no paintings, for the salt air would damage them with time.

Wein suddenly felt someone's gaze. He looked in that direction, spying a girl peeking at him from the shadow of a statue. She looked younger than his sister. He'd never seen her before.

However, he could tell from her clothing that she was of a high rank.

Some kid from a noble family? She must be here to gawk at foreign royalty.

The gears in his mind turned. When he looked in her direction again, she was already gone.

Hmm… Well, whatever.

He was a little curious about her, but his crucial match was waiting just up ahead. He wanted his eyes to stay focused on the prize.

"This is the audience hall."

They finally stood before the door. As the officials solemnly pushed it open, they were met with a lineup of vassals and guards. A large human shadow sat enshrined in the center.

"Welcome, young prince."

Gruyere Soljest.

The ruler of the nation flashed an arrogant smile.

—*I get it now*, Ninym thought to herself upon catching sight of Gruyere.

She stood among the attendants behind Wein.

The palace had to accommodate Gruyere's impressive girth.

He was very husky. Maybe even dreadfully corpulent. Coupled with his height, he was like a rocky boulder resting on the throne. Jiva would look like a pebble next to him.

The fine chair that sagged under him looked like cheap woodwork that might splinter at any moment.

"I'm delighted to receive an invitation to your ceremony, King Gruyere."

Gruyere called out heartily, "Of course! I've been dying to speak with you again after we joined forces to liberate Mealtars. I'm thrilled we could have this opportunity."

"Likewise, King Gruyere. I'm certain this meeting will be fruitful for both of us."

He nodded magnanimously. "I have no doubt. Are you hungry? I prefer to dine while talking with important guests."

Wein looked a little surprised as he shrugged his shoulders. "I'm embarrassed to admit I might have more of an appetite than you."

"Ha-ha-ha! Looks like we have a contender!" Gruyere slapped his jelly belly.

It echoed like a drum.

"I hope your stomach can keep up with that mouth of yours," the king teased. "Our cuisine is first-rate. I imagine you'll eat two—or even three—of your normal servings."

Gruyere raised a single hand. Several men came in carrying a palanquin. Wein balked at him as they rolled the king into it and hoisted it up.

"To the reception hall."

"......"

The men walked with the palanquin as if they were totally used to it. Wein snapped back to his senses and hurried after them.

"What's wrong? Do you find something odd about this?" Gruyere asked from his perch.

Wein chose his words very carefully. "...I was thinking this is a cultural difference."

Gruyere smiled congenially. "I believe I mentioned it's hard to walk around when you look like this. This is my usual mode of transportation."

I see, Wein thought.

He'd assumed the palace had been built to suit Gruyere's size, but it was more accurate to say it had been built to allow him enough space to utilize a palanquin.

"A lifetime of seeking indulgence has caused this figure, if I remember correctly."

"Indeed. Nobility can do what others cannot. Walking on feet is peasant logic. If you are a self-professed person of wealth, you have to get the lower classes to carry you."

"I understand what you are saying, but…"

"I know. Each person of the nobility has a different calling. Maybe yours is different."

"My own calling? I cannot imagine what that might be."

"In youth, we are drawn to many things, lured by temptation. As we repeat failures and successes, we come to face the beast growing inside us and understand what it wants."

Wein thought to himself, *He's one open-minded king…*

When they first met in Cavarin, he'd been overwhelmed by the king's appearance. There was no time for them to interact in Mealtars. However, this laid-back discussion seemed to support his reputation as a wise ruler.

I knew I could trust my gut…! I need to team up with Gruyere!

He assumed Soljest would be after friendly relations. They wanted to curb Natra from advancing west and to band against Delunio.

I thought I'd ask them to let us have a piece of their economic pie by trading with other nations…but I might be able to get more out of this.

In other words, they might be able to form an alliance against Delunio.

The plan would be for Natra and Soljest to work together to topple the kingdom.

Natra has enough soldiers to mobilize. If we attacked a kingdom in the West, Levetia won't stay quiet about it. But Gruyere is a Holy Elite. He can do what he wants. We could destroy Delunio, split up the territory, and establish channels to trade with each other… Man, I hate to toot my own horn, but this is too perfect.

If all went well, the value of their kingdom would shoot skyward. Of course, this was all hypothetical, but Gruyere had been the one to invite him over. He clearly wanted to get along. There was value in taking on the challenge, enough for Wein to take a gamble.

I've got to seal an alliance with Gruyere if it's the last thing I do…!

The party arrived at their destination. Centerpieces and silverware were placed along the table in preparation for a feast.

As Wein scanned the room, his eyes stopped on someone—the young girl in the place of honor…Gruyere's and Wein's seats.

"That's…"

He'd seen her when he entered the palace.

Just as Wein wondered what she was doing here, Gruyere provided an answer.

"Hmph… That's my daughter. Tolcheila."

"Ah, I see, your daughter… Hold up! Your *daughter…*?!"

Wein couldn't help looking back and forth between Gruyere and his daughter. Compared to obesity personified, she was petite and slim and bore virtually no resemblance to him.

"We share the same personality, but she takes after her mother's looks… Tolcheila, what are you doing there? Didn't I say to stay away while we have a special guest?"

Gruyere's tone made it obvious that he had a soft spot for her. He offered a wry smile as if he was happy about this inconvenience.

She knew she had him wrapped around her finger.

Tolcheila puffed out her chest. "I reckon I can't heed your orders, Father."

There was something distinct about her speech pattern.

"It would be a darn shame if I couldn't exchange any words with Prince Wein. I mean, I reckon everyone across this continent knows him. I humbly request to join you."

"Hmph..." Gruyere thought it over. "Ask the prince. If you can get him to agree, you can stay."

What? Since when is this my *job?*

Wein immediately glared at Gruyere as Tolcheila tiptoed over to him and gave him an elegant bow.

"It's a pleasure to meet you, Prince Wein. I'm Tolcheila, the daughter of King Gruyere."

"Thank you, Princess Tolcheila. If my memory serves me right, we had the pleasure of meeting before."

"Ah, you caught me." She didn't seem to express any guilt about spying on him. "They say tact is necessary when making your move... Anyway, I've been curious to find out more about the rumored 'Prince Wein.' Forgive me for my incivility."

"Of course. Don't mention it. Having the attention of a beautiful woman is one of the joys of man."

"That tickles me pink. If you let me join you, my eyes will be all yours. What say you? I know a few things about our cuisine."

Wein thought over her proposal. His top priority was to negotiate with Gruyere. Time was of the essence. It wasn't strategic to spend it on third parties. However, it seemed Gruyere and Tolcheila got along. He was better off winning her over.

And besides...

As someone with a younger sister, how could he turn her down?

"—I could not ask for more," Wein replied. "We feast with our eyes. Besides, I am interested in learning more about your culinary tastes. Please. By all means."

"I knew you'd come around. I won't make you regret this, Prince Wein."

Tolcheila nodded in satisfaction, and the three of them sat in the seats of honor. The banquet began.

If he was being perfectly honest, his expectations for the feast hadn't been very high.

After all, he was royalty. For his entire life, he'd had opportunities to enjoy the finest food. As an exchange student in the Empire and during his trip to Mealtars, he'd gotten a taste of elaborate dishes.

Listen. I'm a prince. Obviously, I've got a refined palate. Best food on the continent? We're in the boonies, dude! It can't be all that different from Natra. Well, I guess they'll make up for it in variety, since they're big traders. I mean, don't get me wrong. I'm obviously interested in discovering new flavors.

Wein held tight to his condescending attitude...for stupid reasons. No one seemed to care about food in Natra, and he didn't want to admit his daily meals kinda sucked.

Food was placed before him.

"For starters, we have a white fish and herb salad."

It was a dish made up of thin slices of white fish decorated with red, green, and yellow vegetables. Tolcheila began to explain.

"Caught in coastal waters, it is a tricky fish to preserve. But it's exquisite when fresh. Give it a taste."

"I will. I mean, freshness is next to godliness," he said, though he looked down on the food in disdain.

What the heck? This is the blandest dish around. I mean, yeah, it looks good. Maybe even really *good. But the best on the continent? They totally raised the bar. I thought it would be fancier. Huh. Total fail. What a letdown!*

Wein ventured to take a bite. He chewed, let it sit on his palate, swallowed, and took a breath.

IT'S DELICIOOOOOOUS! Wein shrieked. Internally.

How in the world? Wait. That's impossible! How can it be this good? But it's just fish! Like regular old sliced-up fish?!

White fish had a subtle taste, but the sauce just seemed to elevate its flavors, and the herbal fragrance tickled his nostrils. They harmonized on the tongue.

"Like it?"

"Y-yes, it's quite delicious..."

Wein panicked inside as he nodded. At this rate, Natra's food would be unanimously voted blandest in the land!

Calm yourself! This is just the first dish! It could have been a miracle. We haven't lost yet...!

Wein devoured the white fish as he rallied himself.

We feast with our eyes! It tastes incredible, but the plating is...meh! The best dishes pay attention to presentation and palate!

"Seems the next course has arrived."

The plate was placed in front of Wein.

Ngh... Th-this is...?!

"A bowl carved from fruit, filled with a delectable mousse made from fish, shellfish, and eggs. Doesn't its presentation just draw the eye?"

Tolcheila was correct. The brilliant orange of the fruit and white mousse inside created a delicious contrast. The top half of the cut fruit served as a decorative lid, making it look like an open treasure chest.

Gah...! I have no choice but to give it a perfect ten...! Well, let me taste it first... Damn it! It's delicious! Make that a twelve!

Unlike the previous dish, the rich taste of seafood almost bloomed in his mouth, and the acidity from the fruit bowl served to cleanse the palate from a greasy aftertaste.

"It appears you're taken by the dish."

"I-indeed. It's perfect down to the details."

Wein internally clutched his head. Did he have no choice but admit his food left a lot to be desired? Did Soljest have no weaknesses for him to prey upon?!

I-it's not over yet! Maybe the plating and flavors are fantastic! But it doesn't make a splash. For a banquet, there needs to be something to make an impact.

"Here's the roast pig."

AAAAAAAH?!

He could smell it from across the room as several servants entered the hall with an iron plate that held a whole pig, plump as fruit. Bubbling oil sizzled, and the delicious aroma filled the room. Its presence was undeniable. *Why does meat taste so good?* it seemed to ask. *Because it's meat, obviously.* Even if he closed his eyes, he couldn't quell his raging appetite.

Even his entourage and the vassals let out sighs of wonder. With all eyes focused on it, the servants began to cut into the pig. Even the fullest stomachs created extra space for it.

As he savored the piece served to him, his stomach spoke of the truth. There was no mincing it. It wasn't necessary. Its flavor profile was more than enough to satisfy the palate.

...I've lost... They have me totally beat... Wein admitted as he ate the roast.

Hauling it in on a steel plate was part of the performance. The

©Falmaro

first two courses had toned things down, so the roast pig could make such an impact. Their attention to detail spoke volumes of their food culture.

"Delicious, right?"

"Very... It lives up to the rumors. It's exquisite."

"We encourage the creation of new and innovative food. We have a designated arena where we can test our skills, and those with potential are granted a reward and title. Talented chefs from across the nation gather in Phithcha to push forward progress. All under my father's leadership."

Right? Tolcheila seemed to ask her father. He stopped eating for a moment. He had enough in front of him to feed a family of five.

"It's no big deal. I was wondering how to devour all the delicious food around the world, and it was too much work to go out there and find it myself. So I conjured up a plan that would incentivize chefs to come here."

"I admire your pursuit of fine cuisine, King Gruyere. If my memory serves me right, don't you see food as the means to an end—to achieve your physique?"

"Indeed. And isn't this the most kingly way to achieve my goal?"

"You're right."

Wein and Gruyere smiled at each other.

Never in my wildest dreams would I have thought their food culture was this advanced.

He was eager to soak up as much knowledge about their cuisine as possible during his stay. He was going to bring it back home and see if he could popularize it. If things worked out, it would make this trip worth it. Wein nodded to himself, and...

...Wait! That's not what I'm here for! he shrieked internally. *I want to team up with Soljest! I mean, their food is awesome! And it'd be great if I could bring it back to Natra! But I don't have time for that right now!*

Wein shuddered. He realized his mind had been overcome with thoughts of food. This cuisine was something to be feared.

"Next course," Tolcheila announced.

"Gah…!"

His thoughts immediately started to turn back to his plate, but Wein caught himself at the last minute.

Pull it together! Our future depends on whether you can make nice with Gruyere! Quit thinking about the meal, even if it's the best thing you've ever had!

He took a breath.

—I refuse to lose to food!

"Plan failed…"

Stuffed to the brim, Wein collapsed on the bed in the room prepared for him.

"Couldn't take your mind off the food, huh," Ninym observed in exasperation.

She was right. Wein had devoured course after course. In the end, not a word of an alliance had been uttered.

"I'm no saint! The food was just so good!"

"I get it…but you ate twice as much as usual. How's your stomach holding up?"

"It hurts…"

"To be expected." Ninym let out a long sigh, rubbing his back. "It'll get better with time. Just lie down… I have to admit I'm surprised. I know you were too focused on the meal, but I didn't expect King Gruyere to bring up nothing."

"Huh… You're right…"

Gruyere had been the one who'd invited Wein on the pretense

of a ceremony. It couldn't be just to eat and chat. He must have had some political motivation in mind.

"Well, we're planning to stay for three days. I guess he doesn't feel the need to rush?" Ninym said.

"I don't think it just slipped his mind… I'll bring it up tomorrow. I mean, all that's on our schedule is the simple ritual for the ceremony in the morning, right?"

"Yes. The opening ceremony is tomorrow, and the closing event is two days after that. I'm sure he'll make time to discuss important matters with us. Try not to lose yourself in the food next time."

He broke into a smile. "Relax. I'm not the type of man to make the same mistake twice."

"This isn't the first time you've given yourself cramps from overeating."

"…Um. I won't make the same mistake twice… Starting now!"

Ninym sighed upon hearing his pathetic attempt at an excuse.

At this point in time, they still had hints of optimism.

Wein was certain Gruyere wanted to talk about political matters.

For good reason, too. Even from an objective standpoint, anyone would expect the countries to deepen their relationship.

Wein had attended the ceremony at the palace, trying to catch Gruyere afterward.

"King Gruyere, might I have a word?"

"Oh, if it isn't the prince. Perfect timing. They just finished prepping some food."

"Um… scrambled eggs mixed with minced vegetables. The two flavor profiles complement each other."

"Exactly. Loved by our commoners. It's also great with potatoes."

"Interesting. I'll be sure to try it once I return home. I would like to talk to you about—"

"Oh, sorry, I've got some business. Let's link up later."

"Huh? Um…"

Gruyere crawled into his palanquin and was whisked away.

…*What?* Wein didn't get it, but he wasn't going to give up.

Having pulled himself together, he tried again at lunchtime.

"Ah, Prince Wein. Thank you for coming," greeted Tolcheila, in Gruyere's stead.

In front of him was the largest mountain of sweets that he'd ever seen.

"I'm obsessed with these. I began baking myself, because I can't get enough. Try this. It's called chocolate. Help yourself."

"It melts in your mouth. What a strange sensation. And the aroma is very unique. I understand why you've taken a liking to it, Princess Tolcheila."

"Right? I take seeds picked in the South, crush them into a fine powder, then mix that with milk and butter. I'm having our chefs research other possible uses."

"I would love to bring some back for my younger sister… By the way, would you happen to know where King Gruyere might be?"

"My father, hm? Weight as heavy as a boulder, heart as light as a feather. Who can say what he's up to? Well, I'm certain he'll return soon enough. Here. Try this one."

Wein stayed behind, chatting with her while he waited for Gruyere, but the king never showed up.

…*What?*

Even though Wein was eager to form an alliance, he just never seemed to get ahold of Gruyere.

Not that it stopped him from trying.

Huh—?!

Wein didn't exchange another word with King Gruyere on that day.

"—That's weird."

Sitting in a chair in his room, Wein crossed his arms and looked at the ceiling.

"It gave me pause yesterday, but we still haven't gotten a chance to meet today. Something has to be going on."

Ninym responded with a troubled look. "Maybe he's trying to avoid us?"

"……"

That seemed to be a reasonable conclusion. But why?

Their relationship with Delunio was coming apart at the seams. Soljest would win if they fought one-on-one. But if Natra joined hands with their enemy? Who knows what would happen?

That was why they had invited Wein to Soljest—to form ties with Natra. At least, Wein had imagined that was the case.

However, Gruyere was defying all expectations, avoiding any attempt at discussion. He just didn't seem like someone who wanted to strengthen relations.

Maybe he has no plans to team up with Natra…? You would think pulling us away from Delunio would be high up on their priorities list…

He couldn't get a read on the situation. Right now, it was the only conclusion he could draw.

Let's say that's the case. Why am I here? It can't just be that he wanted to show off his food and shoot the breeze with me.

Maybe if they were good friends. However, they were officials with limited time on their schedules. It would be a waste to invite Wein to a ceremony and do nothing but eat. They hadn't even had a single decent conversation.

Why would King Gruyere invite a prince with no interest in forming an alliance?

—Assassination.

That was at the forefront of his mind.

Natra was making strides, which meant Soljest had to be feeling the heat. They could be scheming to assassinate Wein to freeze their progress.

...But would he follow through with that? I mean, he is a Holy Elite, but his reputation will plummet if he murders the prince of a foreign nation.

Wein had killed Ordalasse, the king of Cavarin and another member of the Holy Elite. He had passed the blame onto one of the king's generals and escaped censure, but he found it hard to believe Gruyere would be able to worm himself out of this one. Even if he made it look like an accident, the scandal would reach the far corners of the continent, giving him no escape.

Plus...he already had his chance to kill me. Why is he dallying...?

It hit Wein instantly.

To extend my stay...and buy time...! How am I disadvantaged by staying here...?

"By being away from Natra...!" Wein sprang up from his chair, startling Ninym.

"Wh-what's wrong, Wein?"

"That pig! He's scheming to do something to Natra in my absence... He might have even started to make his move...!"

At this point, it was just a guess, a theory, a hypothesis. However, he couldn't afford to be careless now.

"Ninym! Prepare to head back! Tell everyone to be on standby for my order!"

"—Understood!" Ninym was ready to dash out of the room, quelling her momentary confusion.

That was when someone knocked on his door.

"Please pardon me. May I come in, Prince Wein?"

Ninym and Wein exchanged a look. He gave the tiniest of nods. She opened the door with a concealed knife, ready to strike at any moment.

"I apologize for stopping by at this hour, Prince Wein."

Tolcheila stood outside the door, accompanied by an attendant.

"...Princess Tolcheila, what can I do for you this late in the evening? You haven't come for a secret rendezvous, I imagine."

She smiled. "Sounds fun, but I'm here for something else. Father has finally finished wrapping up his duties. He would like to know if he can have the pleasure of your company for a glass of wine. I'll be there, too." She looked proud.

"I see." Wein's mind raced.

Did I jump to the wrong conclusion...? But I should assume the worst. If Gruyere is up to something, I should—

He faced Tolcheila, offering a smile. "I have no reason to decline a direct invitation from King Gruyere. I would be delighted to join him."

"Wonderful. Let us be on our way." She triumphantly led them toward where her father was waiting.

He whispered to Ninym, observing Tolcheila from behind. "Tell the others that they might bar us from leaving or there might be war. They need to be prepared."

Wein had to get in touch with Gruyere first. When the time came, he couldn't let the king know he was suspicious of his motivations...

at least, not until Wein could ask about the alliance and find out his true intentions.

If all worked out, great. But if Gruyere refused—

"We might have to take Tolcheila or Gruyere hostage and flee the city," he whispered.

"I'll make sure we're ready." Ninym nodded.

Wein followed after Tolcheila, fingers running over the weapon concealed beneath his clothes.

"There you are."

Gruyere was waiting in the corner of a moonlit balcony.

"Forgive me for my actions this afternoon. I had to attend to other guests."

"Don't mention it. As a politician, I'm all too familiar with unexpected events cropping up."

As Wein sat down across from Gruyere, Tolcheila took a seat next to her father. Wein thought they had positioned themselves at a distance from him.

But if necessary, I can take them on...

Gruyere was the pillar of this nation. And Tolcheila, his darling daughter.

Either one would make an adequate hostage. There was a good chance Gruyere was up to something, so he had to be ready to move at any time.

Gruyere suddenly said something out of the blue.

"We have empty seats. Hey, servant. Yes, you. Come and sit down."

"Ah... Me?" Ninym answered from behind Wein.

She had already finished relaying Wein's orders, trailing behind him like a shadow.

This threw her off her game.

"Um. I'm honored you have called upon me…but…"

She was being cagey for obvious reasons.

Although this was not an official setting, it was rare for the king of one nation to call upon the servant of another. As a Flahm, she knew standing before him would only cause problems.

No one would have guessed what he would say next.

"I've heard about the prince's favorite Flahm. It's fine. I don't fuss over the petty things."

All were floored, including his daughter. He'd asked Ninym to join them despite knowing she was a Flahm. It was unimaginable for the king of a Western nation to show such tolerance.

"…Well then, I shall join you."

He left her no option to refuse. She perched in a seat next to Wein.

"Very good… What's wrong, Prince? Are you surprised?"

"…Pardon my rudeness, but yes. This may be the first time in history that a follower of Levetia—and Holy Elite—has invited a Flahm to sit with them."

"Heh. It seems I've initiated a historic moment unintentionally." Gruyere jovially emptied his glass.

"The scriptures state the Flahm are the devil's messenger. Don't you think your request is sacrilegious?"

"The scriptures!" Gruyere cried, jiggling his stomach. "You must know, Prince Wein, that those scraps have been rewritten to suit the interests of the few."

"We've experienced that firsthand in Natra."

Wein was talking about the Circulous Law.

The new interpretation of the text came from conspiring jurists, nixing Natra from the pilgrimage. It had been backed by the Holy Elites during that time.

"The people want scripture. For what? For answers. They want to know the right way to live up to God's expectations, guarantee peace in the afterlife, and you know the rest. They're grateful for the model answers provided in the papers, which have been revised by generations of Holy Elites."

"But without it, the people will fumble around in the darkness."

"*That's fine*," Gruyere said declaratively. "We must think for ourselves and find our own answers as to whether we're living up to divine expectations or on the right path. It isn't an easy path, but there's no shortcut when it comes to God."

"Is that how you came to the conclusion that Flahm are humans, too?"

"Indeed. As a king, all my subjects are equal. What does it matter if their hair is white or their eyes red?" Gruyere beamed.

Next to him, Tolcheila chimed in, sounding curious. "Did you dye your hair?"

"Y-yes."

"Looks good."

The princess seemed to talk to Ninym like anyone else. Like father, like daughter.

"I understand your point, King Gruyere." Wein was choosing his words carefully. "But would God approve of your running with this interpretation?"

"I'll cross that bridge when I come to it," he countered. "To rest on God's knee or to burn in the flames of hell. If I can only experience one, I'd say they're both valuable experiences. God is the only one who can deliver this final judgment. Not scripture. Not sermons."

"......"

He's tough, Wein honestly thought, overcome with admiration.

King Gruyere wasn't even from the East. He was the king of a Western nation and a Holy Elite at that. For him to hold this opinion was considered peculiar, to say the least.

The main takeaway wasn't his morality or ethics, but the conviction behind his words and actions. Wein knew the king's heart would not break even on the verge of death.

There was another thing that he noticed in Gruyere.

The pig has no openings...!

He was twice as fat as the average person. A literal mass of blubber. He didn't have any militancy in him...or he hadn't had it... until just a while ago.

Now there was something different about him. Sitting in his custom chair, he was like a man-eating bear preparing for battle. His eyes continued to seize Wein and Ninym, threatening to swing his arm down on them if they moved too quickly.

Think about it. We've got to be faster than him if we're lighter...

However, Wein couldn't make his move. There was instinct holding him back, even though logic was trying to argue otherwise. King Gruyere was a real menace.

Extending an invitation to Ninym hadn't been on an inebriated whim. It was a calculated move to slow her movements by keeping her seated and within range. Wein and Ninym had planned to take either Gruyere or Tolcheila as a live hostage, but it seemed the king had other plans.

Move, and I'll kill you or murder your servant, he seemed to imply.

"...King Gruyere, I admire your personhood and individuality. There is no country I would rather join hands with."

Under the tense air, Wein challenged Gruyere with a glare.

"It seems we're experiencing problems in Natra. I know the ceremony is only halfway finished, but I'm afraid we must return home immediately. Before that, I wish to form friendly relations between Natra and Soljest to weather through these tumultuous times. What do you say?"

Wein was certain the king would reject the offer.

Gruyere had caught him in a trap. Based on the king's attitude, he must have known Wein had unraveled his plan. He might have even had the palace surrounded by armed soldiers.

Our only exit strategy is to strike first.

He exchanged a look with Ninym and judged his timing. As the pressure mounted, Gruyere got ready to speak, taking his time.

"Sounds good. I accept."

"...Excuse me?" Wein blinked.

Ninym followed suit.

The king smiled at Wein. "What's wrong, Prince? Did I catch you off guard?"

"Um... You're going to accept?"

"My word is my bond. Of course, we'll need to iron out the details. We can't make it official right away, so I hope you're fine with a verbal agreement. But an alliance sounds splendid. Right, Tolcheila?"

"Agreed. Very auspicious."

What—?!

This threw Wein off his game.

Are you seriously going to say yes?! And here I was, certain we were heading for war! Not that I'm complaining!

"What's wrong, Prince? Your expressions are looking...funny."

"I-it's nothing. I'm so happy, I do not know what to do with myself."

"Savor the moment... Oh, I guess you have to hurry back to your homeland, right?"

"Y-yes, well..."

That had been his excuse to strong-arm Gruyere into giving an answer, but he couldn't just go back on his word: *"Actually, I'm thinking of staying, now that we've formed an alliance. Your food is delicious, by the way."* Yeah. No chance.

"In that case, I won't delay you any longer. We can discuss the details of the alliance by communicating through our subordinates. Tolcheila, see that the prince is sent off."

"Understood." She stood up.

Gruyere was essentially setting her up to be their hostage. That had to be part of his plan. Maybe it was a sign of his cooperation?

In any case, they had accomplished what they set out to do. Now everything would fall into place…if they could get home safely.

"I'm grateful for your hospitality, King Gruyere. I'll be sure to repay you one day."

"I'll expect a thank-you gift that will astound me. Farewell, Crown Prince."

Guided by Tolcheila, Wein bowed, leaving the balcony with Ninym in tow.

Gruyere was now all alone.

"I'm interested to see how this performance turns out," he murmured before looking toward the corner of the balcony.

That figure hadn't been there moments before.

"—Don't you agree, Sir Sirgis?"

"Yes, King Gruyere."

Sirgis. The prime minister of Delunio offered a superficial smile and nodded.

As instructed, their entourage had prepared to return home. Ninym conducted a final check as Wein bowed to Tolcheila.

"Thank you for coming to bid us farewell, Princess Tolcheila. I'm terribly sorry we're leaving so suddenly. I wish we could have had more time together."

"Worry not. Our time might have been brief, but I got a good idea of who you are."

"Yeah? And what would that be?"

"Well..." Tolcheila thought for a moment. "I would say you are an intelligent, courageous, and fascinating liar."

"A liar, huh? And here I thought my double tongue had lost some function by savoring your food."

"Hee-hee. You're in interesting one. Won't you take me as your wife? In a few years, I'm sure you won't be able to take your eyes off my body."

"...I shall take your offer home with me and consider it."

"What? Do you fancy a certain lass? Well, let's discuss it when you visit the next time."

"I'm not sure when there will be a 'next time.'"

They were both the royalty of other nations, after all. Their opportunities to meet were few and far between.

Tolcheila lowered her voice so no one else could hear. "Sooner than you think."

"What was that?"

"Ah, nothing. I was talking to myself." She smiled. "Farewell, Prince Wein. I pray for your safe journey."

"Thank you. Until next time, Princess Tolcheila."

Wein climbed into the carriage, and they left the moonlit palace. They remained cautious of assassins while on the road, but the party returned to Natra without incident.

However, respite lasted only a moment. Wein received two pieces of unexpected news.

First, Delunio and Marden were engaging in combat at the border.

Second, in light of these incidents, Soljest had declared war on Natra as part of their treaty with Delunio.

It all started when a letter from Delunio arrived in Marden after Wein's departure.

The message was simple: Their new territory contained a piece of land that Delunio had loaned to the royal family of Marden indefinitely. However, when the kingdom fell, this agreement became null and void, meaning the plot had to be returned immediately.

"That's ridiculous," Zenovia said upon receiving this letter, rejecting it without a second thought.

They did possess loaned land, but this agreement had been made decades prior. At the time, Marden had wanted to purchase the territory, but Delunio had forced them into calling it an indefinite loan instead. There was no reason why they would give it back, especially now.

Zenovia sent them a polite version of *Don't ever show your face here again*, which Delunio must have expected because their response was lightning fast.

"Lady Zenovia, we have reports of an army near the border we share with Delunio."

They investigated soon after hearing the news and confirmed them to be Delunio soldiers as expected. The army was there under the pretext of training, but it was obvious they were pressuring Marden with militaristic force in response to their previous reply.

"Borgen, lead the troops and head to the location. Refrain from engaging in unnecessary battle."

"Understood."

She wasn't overreacting by deploying her troops. If she tried to negotiate, it would have demonstrated she would yield to military force, which would make her the subject of future scorn.

Besides, I doubt they want conflict.

It was just their way of saying they wanted to talk things over again, Zenovia thought. Their relationship with Soljest was rocky, and it wouldn't be strategic to go to war against Natra.

At this moment in time, she didn't know she was in the palm of Delunio's hand.

Soon after, she received reports of Delunio crossing the border, giving rise to battles to stop the enemy from advancing.

As if hounding them for an answer, Soljest made a sudden declaration of war.

"This is—"

Zenovia finally realized she'd fallen for their trap...

Soljest had declared war.

In Natra, the top brass buzzed around like angered bees in a prodded hive.

Although they'd won against Marden and Cavarin, Soljest was on another level, and they knew it. With a surprise attack coming from them, they were obviously going to be agitated.

Even so, they weren't going to spiral out of control or fall into despair...because of someone right before their eyes.

Their young crown prince. Their emotional support. A future hero destined to be a part of history.

"Have we gathered the home forces?"

"About eighty percent have arrived in the capital. We should have everyone in two days."

"And where are the men of Soljest?"

"There have been recent reports that they have crossed the border. Based on the speed of their advance, we believe their forces are approaching the Trost grasslands soon."

"Pick up the pace, and organize the troops! Don't forget the food rations!"

"Sir!"

"As for a concrete battle plan—"

Wein called out orders to his vassals, who were in awe of his composure and certainty.

"I should have expected he would remain steadfast even in these most trying of times."

"I was wrong to lose myself when I heard the declaration of war. I'm ashamed of myself."

"Get over it. It's only a matter of time before we find glory on the battlefield."

The war council paused for a break as the vassals chatted among themselves.

As if waiting for this opportunity, Ninym whispered in Wein's ear.

"Your Highness, I believe now would be a good time for you to rest."

Wein nodded, standing up. "I will be in my office. Call if anything happens."

"Understood."

After the officers saw them off, Wein returned to his office with Ninym. As soon as she closed the door, he sucked in a deep breath…

"—CURSE THAT DAMN PIG!"

His wails rang through the office.

"Screw him! Accepting my offer? How dare he! He must have realized we'd try to kill him if he rejected me, which is why he ran his mouth! A verbal agreement? That means nothing! Damn it! He got me!"

Wein could never show this side of himself to his vassals. Ninym looked troubled.

"Who could have guessed that Soljest and Delunio would form an alliance…?"

"You're telling me…! Damn it! It wasn't just Gruyere. Sirgis got me, too…!"

Sirgis and Gruyere must have been conspiring while Wein was in Marden. Or they had already come up with this plan by that point.

Wein imagined Gruyere chuckling to himself as he celebrated his little victory. He felt like kicking something.

"Gruyere invited you to the ceremony with the intention of forming an alliance. Sirgis interfered before you arrived and persuaded the king to join him instead. By the time you got there, they'd already mapped out the plan… That's your proposed timeline, right?"

"Yeah, I don't think it's too far off, though I'm not even sure if he intended to band with us in the first place."

"You think he was planning to fight us from the beginning?"

"Just based on his behavior. Even when he first invited me, I didn't think it was to form friendly relations. I thought it was to evaluate his enemy or something."

"If that's the case, the two nations must have formed a secret alliance before he invited you… I suppose the details don't really matter."

Soljest and Delunio had joined forces to make an enemy of his nation. In other words, Natra had failed to resolve this with diplomacy. They had to suck it up and come up with a game plan.

"We've got no choice but to gather our forces and fight Soljest. It'll be hard to face them head-on. That's why we need to make one more move."

"And the missing piece of that puzzle..." Ninym started to say when someone knocked on the door. An officer.

"Your Highness, please excuse the interruption. The marquess of Marden has just arrived."

"Understood. Show her in."

"Yes!" The official disappeared through the door.

"The ace up our sleeve is here."

"...I wonder if Zenovia will be all right."

"I think I know how she's feeling...but see for yourself." Wein grinned. "We've got no time for tears. Even if her heart's broken, I'll get her moving. Just wait."

As the official guided her to the office, Zenovia felt as if she were a criminal heading to her execution.

This was because the upcoming war with Soljest had been a chain reaction of the fight between Delunio and Marden.

But I never thought it would come to this...

For Zenovia, it was a horrific nightmare. She'd jumped into a carriage upon receiving Wein's summons, and her face had been pale for the entire journey.

The color still hadn't returned to her face, even after she arrived at the palace. In fact, as the flurry of officials and nobility took notice of her and whispered among themselves, her complexion turned even more ghastly. She wished she could run away or turn to stone.

Even so, that would obviously be unforgivable. After all, she was the lord of the territory.

There are still things I can do...! Trembling as she rebuked herself, Zenovia realized she was in front of the door.

"Your Highness, I have brought Marquess Zenovia."

"Come in."

Wein's voice sounded grimmer than usual, but maybe she was imagining things. Zenovia stepped into the office.

"Thank you for coming... I can see you understand the gravity of the situation."

"...I'm so sorry, Prince Wein!" Zenovia immediately fell to her knees. "My stupid response to Delunio is to blame! I offer no excuses!"

Wein nodded when he heard her heartfelt apology. He probably could have scolded her, but he didn't waste any time, continuing detachedly.

"Lady Zenovia, have you been filled in on the situation?"

"Y-yes. Soljest is leading fifteen thousand soldiers from the West..."

"That's right. Natra was able to gather eight thousand men. Though we're facing some delays, we're hoping to add another three thousand, which would leave us at eleven thousand. We just don't have enough people."

Their foe was Gruyere, the famed battle leader.

Though Natra had General Hagal, he wouldn't make up for the difference. Even if they could engage in a fair fight, they were about to face major damages. Natra would become prey for another nation as their army recovered. Frankly speaking, the situation put them in jeopardy.

"...I already came to my decision on the way here. I am prepared to accept any manner of punishment," Zenovia said with a grave expression.

It looked like shame, frustration, worthlessness were devouring her whole. However, she managed to keep her feelings at bay.

"I wish for the opportunity to redeem myself."

—*Huh*, Wein thought to himself.

Zenovia had thrown him for a loop.

I figured she'd be a total mess.

Wein had never intended on holding her responsible. Marden would only grow more agitated if he punished her and broke down their leader. And honestly, they didn't have enough human capital to afford that.

Furthermore, he didn't think she was wrong in responding to Delunio in this way. It was unreasonable to expect her to predict Soljest would wage war.

Even if she wasn't wrong, a mistake was a mistake. It was bad enough that Marden had earned jealousy as the newest territory. Inviting war put Zenovia in a precarious position.

On top of that, he doubted she could handle the pressure. He'd never expected her to say she wished to make up for it.

"And how do you plan on redeeming yourself?"

"By restoring harmony with Delunio," she offered. "Soljest declared war because we threatened their ally. If Delunio and Natra can reconcile, Soljest will have no justification to attack…!"

Zenovia knew she was going to die as soon as they waged war.

Her throat would be slit. There was no way around it. Right now, she was thinking of ways that the enemy would be satisfied with just her head—all to prevent her household from being stripped of its title. The situation called for it.

She had asked her vassals to refine this plan before she made her way to the palace—but their response was different from hers. They sought a solution that would ensure her survival.

She didn't ask why. As she gazed at their stern profiles, she knew she couldn't be so insensitive. She was ashamed she'd accepted death as inevitable and joined in their discussion.

There was the tiniest chance of achieving reconciliation with Delunio. If successful, it would give them the greatest chance of saving Zenovia and her household.

"We might be able to stop Soljest. But will Delunio actually be willing to talk?"

"That will be no issue. Jiva is leading the other vassals to Delunio. We've already arranged a meeting with Sirgis."

When Marden had still been a kingdom, they facilitated discussions between Soljest and Delunio. They had used the favor owed to its advantage.

"Of course, I expect it will be difficult to resolve our differences. I have a plan to carry us through it. I ask you to give me a chance…!" Zenovia appealed to him as if it were a prayer.

It was true she had devised her own plan. However, without his permission to execute it, she would die.

Life or death. Zenovia's stomach churned.

"…I'm surprised," Wein suddenly murmured. She raised her head. "I can't believe you already carried out my orders before I gave them to you. Now we can go ahead of schedule."

He turned to Ninym. "We'll head to Delunio right away. Make sure we're ready."

"Understood." She quickly departed the room.

Zenovia watched all of this. "U-um, well, that is…"

"We don't have time to point fingers. I personally don't think the blame is on you. Convince the vassals before this is over, and your sentence will be lighter. You can do it, right, Zenovia?"

"Y-yes!!"

Wein nodded in satisfaction and grinned.

"Let's go. We're about to turn everything upside down."

Fifteen thousand soldiers methodically marched through the swaying grass of the plains. It was the army of Soljest, coming to invade Natra.

Leading the troops was King Gruyere, sitting in a chariot at the forefront.

They'd already broken through the border. Soljest was slowly wedging into Natra like a thorn, and there hadn't been much resistance so far. Natra had to be busy gathering its forces.

"—Your Majesty." A soldier on horseback drew close to the chariot—one of Soljest's generals. "We appear to be progressing without incident."

"Looks that way. I figured the prince would have something up his sleeve, but I guess he ran out of time… Disappointing, really." Gruyere yawned, letting out a beastly groan.

The general went on. "Is it true Delunio isn't going to supply troops?"

On paper, Soljest was just supporting Delunio, which was under attack from Natra. Yet Gruyere's troops were the only ones invading Wein's kingdom.

"This is an excellent opportunity to attack Natra on two fronts. If they aren't mobilizing, we have to wonder if Delunio even intends to take out Natra…"

"Who cares?" Gruyere asked nonchalantly. "All they had to do was provide a 'justified' reason for two eyesore nations to take each other out. What more could Delunio ask for?"

"But as a Holy Elite, you could have waged war in Natra without a reason to do it. We're at a disadvantage in this situation..."

"That's fine," Gruyere asserted. "Thinking is for losers, especially if you're trying to guess the enemy's plans. I am your king, the one who smites every foe—Gruyere."

His composure caused the general to bow. "You're right, Your Majesty. Forgive my needless questioning."

"I forgive you," Gruyere replied, nodding generously.

I doubt Sirgis will stop at Soljest and Natra. He has bigger plans than running us to the ground.

The king knew Sirgis was surprisingly crafty. He had to be, considering he'd climbed the social ladder from commoner to prime minister.

Whatever his methods, he's plotting something after the battle with Natra.

Gruyere looked like he could hardly wait.

He lived for battle and considered it one of the many pleasures in life. This stream of foes was worth more than a mountain of gold.

"The troops of Delunio are weak. Had they joined us, they would have tripped us up," the general offered.

"Uh-huh. And we'd have to give them a chunk of any new territory we acquire. We're better off without them."

The general smiled in agreement.

A messenger came racing toward them on horseback. "I have a report! Scouts have spotted forces from Natra!"

"How many soldiers?"

"Between seven and eight thousand!"

The messenger and the general began to talk between themselves.

Gruyere interrupted. "Did you see the prince's flag?"

"No confirmation on that front, but..."

"Hmph. Has he gone to win over Sirgis...?"

What a waste, Gruyere thought. Reconciling with Delunio would be a brilliant move to halt his troops, but it was hard to imagine Wein would be able to convince Sirgis. The prince would come up empty, and Gruyere would lose his opportunity to battle him. A lose-lose, if you asked him.

"I guess the unexpected brings the fun to the battlefield."

He seemed to be the only one who was satisfied.

Gruyere spoke to his general. "Tell the entire army. As soon as we arrive at our destination, get into formation and prepare for battle."

"Understood!"

Watching his general carry out orders in his periphery, Gruyere dispelled thoughts of Wein from his mind and concentrated on the upcoming fight with Natra.

"...So, those are the troops of Soljest?" Raklum murmured as he observed the battle-ready enemy forces from a distant hill.

Behind him, his own men were prepared, too. They numbered around eight thousand.

"Our opponent stands at fifteen thousand. Twice as many as us. The difference is clear as day."

A man stood next to Raklum. Borgen, the military commander of Marden. "I thought I could earn some glory in this dead-end post. I never thought I'd get tossed onto this hellhole. I would turn tail if I had one."

"Be grateful you don't. If you had turned your back on me, I would have killed you."

"Yeah? It seems the prince thinks highly of you, but are you sure you have the skill to take me on?"

"Without question. If you were my opponent, I would do you in with my fist."

Raklum and Borgen glared at each other before snorting and breaking into a smile. For men of the battlefield, a verbal fistfight was basically a greeting.

"Enough joking around. You know the plan, right, Borgen?"

"Of course. Do you think it'll work?"

"Our prince's orders are never wrong. All we have to do is carry them out."

"Sheesh. Even more loyal than the rumors, huh." Borgen flashed him a wry smile and turned on his heel. "Well, let's do one last check. Don't screw up, Raklum."

"I don't want to hear it from you."

Raklum stared at the enemy army.

The battle was about to begin.

"Everything is ready, Your Majesty."

"Fantastic." Gruyere nodded graciously, looking out at the lineup of over ten thousand soldiers. He appeared before them in his chariot, addressing them in a booming voice.

"Answer me! Who is this man that stands before you?!"

The soldiers shouted back in unison. """"The king of beasts! The ruler of all the land!""""

Gruyere howled back at them. "Answer me! Who are you?"

""""Your fangs! The maw of the beast that rips apart the earth!""""

He lifted his halberd and used it to point toward their adversaries.

"Look, my fangs! Feast your eyes on our prey! Your body trembles with the anticipation of battle! Your blood is boiling at the appearance of a formidable enemy!"

He took a breath. "Rejoice, my fangs! It's the battle you've been waiting for!"

""""RAAAAAAAAAAH!""""

Their war cry shook the earth. They had reached peak morale. Before this had a chance to cool, the commanders assigned to each area started to bark out their orders.

"All units, move out!"

Gruyere's army raced forward in a rallying cry toward Natra.

"Well, I wonder how they'll react."

Now in the rear, Gruyere looked at the backs of his soldiers, gazing at the enemy army up ahead.

They weren't even on the same playing field. The other side realized they had no chance to win in a fair fight. They had to have some kind of strategy if they were taking on the enemy.

Gruyere concentrated on the front lines, trying to probe out their little scheme.

In that instant, unfamiliar forces flanked him, caging him in. The king's eyes widened.

"We'll kill Gruyere. That's the first thing on our list."

Those were Wein's orders to Raklum's team before their departure.

"Understood." Though Raklum had no objections, he did have questions. "May I ask why?"

Wein nodded, motioning to the documents in his hand. "I looked into Gruyere's combat experience and noticed he has a habit of starting each battle in a certain way: brute force. Only after he gets a feel for his opponent does he start issuing orders."

"Do you think that will happen this time?"

"Seems likely. His army is experienced and powerful, and he has the advantage. If we get caught up in his momentum, we could be in trouble."

"Which is why we should aim to strike while he's weaponizing the entire army, leaving him totally defenseless..."

"Exactly. We know the intimate details of the physical location. I've estimated their placement based on the speed of their advance to lay out our attack." Wein continued. "This is a dangerous mission... Can you do it, Raklum?"

He bowed. "Trust me. As your sword, I shall sever the king's head from his body—"

All my exits are blocked off!

Two units had launched a pincher attack against Gruyere. Each team had two hundred soldiers, led by Raklum and Borgen.

It was a lightning attack composed of their most elite forces and carried out at the very last second to avoid detection. Though it was simple enough to explain, its execution was a near-impossible undertaking.

It required extensive knowledge of the terrain, trust in their fellow soldiers, and determination to wait for the enemy to pass by and secure the right position to attack.

However, they had succeeded. Raklum's loyalty to Wein and Borgen's desire to save Zenovia motivated them enough to see through this plan.

"What?! What's going on?!"

"I-it's the enemy! It's an attack! Protect His Majesty!"

The two units launched a barrage of attacks against Gruyere's forces as they tightened their formation around him. Raklum sliced his way through the confused soldiers, closing in on the king. In the opposite direction, Borgen could be seen nocking an arrow and aiming it at his head.

"For His Highness—"

"For the princess—"

The two generals saw their chance.

""I'll have your head!""

Borgen's arrow shot out, booming like a clap of thunder, and Raklum's sword whizzed through the air.

"—Anyone can learn technique and theory."

There was a shrill metallic wail. Raklum's and Borgen's eyes widened in shock.

"If it's conditional on peak physique and focus, it's second rate. You need something that's achievable by anyone—women, children, elderly, even masses of fat… Now that's considered an excellent skill."

An unbelievably shrewd move. Gruyere handled his halberd as if it were a piece of wood, cutting down the arrow flying at him and halting Raklum's blow.

"Did you think this body kept me from moving around? Don't underestimate me, General. Just because I've got a portly figure doesn't mean I can't use the dueling strategies of the royal family."

"NGH—AAAAAAH?!"

Gruyere gave his halberd a full swing, sending Raklum away. The two put some distance between each other. The king seemed to be weary of Borgen. He gestured to his own neck.

"Love an adrenaline rush. You have my praise. But as you can see, my head is still attached."

"…It's too early to let down your guard, King Gruyere. This isn't over yet." Raklum readied his sword.

The king gave a hearty hoot. "Excellent! Now that's what I'm taking about! Go ahead and rip off my armor of ego—!"

Raising up a war cry, Raklum and Gruyere crashed into each other.

Wein's team made their carriage go as fast as it could and reached the capital of Delunio. Jiva had arrived ahead of time as an ambassador, greeting them in front of their prepared lodgings.

"I've been expecting you, Prince Wein, Lady Zenovia." He bowed deeply.

"How's the situation looking?" Wein asked.

"As I mentioned before, I have managed to set up a meeting with the prime minister, though I get the impression he's hostile."

"Not surprising."

It would have been extraordinary if he'd thought highly of Marden after their initial meeting.

Jiva spoke in hushed tones. "Upon further investigation, it appears the leaders of Delunio are dissatisfied with the policies of the prime minister. He might be acting in his own interest."

"What? Are you implying he negotiated with Soljest on his own?" Zenovia asked.

Jiva nodded. "As you are aware, Soljest and Delunio have been fighting for many years, which is rooted in their sovereigns and subjects. Although the prime minister has gained sufficient power, the sudden alliance has shaken their citizens, and the vassals are resentful that their opinions have been slighted."

"Hmm...which means he did it, though he could guess how they would react." Wein thought for a moment. "Well, whatever. Like our army serving out there on the battlefield, we have a job to do. Jiva, how is the plan coming along?"

"The meeting is scheduled for tomorrow afternoon at the palace."

"Tomorrow, huh..." Wein considered this for a moment. "Perfect timing..."

"Your Highness?"

"Nothing. Ninym, get as much info as you can on the discord between the prime minister and the people. Lady Zenovia and Jiva will decide how we want the meeting to go with me."

On Wein's orders, they set out to prepare for the following day.

Meanwhile, on the other side of things...

"Sirgis, why aren't we supplying any troops?"

They were in the audience hall of the palace in Delunio. Sitting upon the throne was the king. Sirgis was bowing before him.

"This is the perfect opportunity for us," the king insisted. "Soljest is invading Natra. Shouldn't we be leading our armies in aid?"

He was in his mid-thirties. There was something about his expression that housed anxiety, irritation, and pain.

"With all due respect, Your Majesty, this isn't the time," Sirgis replied courteously. "You're right that we could do a number on Natra if we mobilized our troops now. But this would mean less blood will be spilled from the troops of Soljest. For this matter, it is crucial that both nations wear themselves out. We ought to remain in place and watch over the battle."

"A-ah...I-is that so...?" The king's face made it clear he wasn't entirely convinced. He looked at Sirgis.

The prime minister hated him for walking on eggshells around his subordinates. Even so, he had no plan to criticize the king. After all, Sirgis was the one who had taught him to behave that way.

From the moment the king was born, Sirgis hadn't allowed him to think for himself, forcing him to indulge in pleasure and escape his duties. As a result, he'd regressed into the type of person who couldn't handle even daily necessities by himself, much less politics.

"Th-then we'll mobilize after the two armies are done fighting, right?"

"Depends on the outcome of the battle. If they're suitably worn down, it's possible."

"I see... That's fine. If they are up against Natra, it won't be easy for Soljest. If our army uses that moment to rush in, we'll be able to take them both down—and become the alphas of the North...!"

"...Well then, I have to review reports from our messengers."

"Very good. You may leave."

Sirgis bowed as he excused himself from the king's presence, followed by his minions.

When they were a distance away from the reception hall, Sirgis murmured, "Two broken nations, huh. I wish."

"Do you think one of them will win? Are we betting on Soljest?"

"Most likely. I'm familiar with their kingdom and Gruyere," Sirgis answered, nodding at his subordinate's question. "After all, Natra is a third-rate nation that has flowed with the tide. Up against the Beast King, there's little chance of their success. I mean, it would be nice if they did a number on Soljest, but I'm keeping my expectations low."

He shook his head. "I hate that the king and military officials are keeping our forces on standby in case of some golden opportunity. All it's done is add to our expenses," he spat before switching topics.

"Once messengers arrive with news of Soljest's overwhelming victory, no one will be able to suggest we interfere. What do you have to report?"

"There are a number of items."

The subordinates flipped through their papers.

"As expected, there has been no stopping the flow of products made in Natra. The clothing seems popular among youth," said one.

"It's even starting to affect the sales of our domestic products," added another. "There have been several incidents of confrontation between the progressive youth and conservatives."

"That pest..." Sirgis clicked his tongue, scorning Natra. "If Soljest takes them down, they won't be able to do commerce so easily. That's when we'll make our move."

"In addition, there has been a wave of protest letters from the nobility over the revised tax system a few days ago. There have been reports of deteriorating health as of late."

"Hmph, sounds like signs of an epidemic. Keep an eye on the town, and immediately file a report if the situation appears to be getting worse. As for the letters... Leave only the necessary ones in my office. Burn the rest."

"Consider it done. Next—" The male subordinate was at a loss for a moment. "I would like to remind you of your meeting with the messengers from Natra tomorrow. We've received word that the prince of Natra and marquess of Marden have arrived at the capital."

Sirgis nodded. Wein had used a favor owed to Marden to set up a meeting, but it would all be in vain.

"I imagine they're hoping to put a halt to our moral cause by pacifying us... Hmph. I can't wait to see them beg me through their tears."

The battle continued to unfold between Natra and Soljest. Another fight was about to break out in a place far removed from the front lines—with big implications for their futures.

The next day, Wein and Zenovia were led to a room in the royal palace. Several officials and a petite elderly man awaited them. It was the prime minister of Delunio, Sirgis.

"I appreciate your willingness to meet us on such short notice, Sir Sirgis." Wein placed his hand against his chest.

"Don't mention it. I've recently imposed on you, so consider us even." He offered a smile, though Zenovia sensed his eyes were dark with scorn. "It's a great honor to have you visit our nation. How can I help you? With all that's going on between Delunio and Natra, I imagine you aren't stopping by without reason."

"You're right," Zenovia cut in. "The war between our nations rose from the issue between our territory and your land. We have come to seek an amicable solution."

"Ah, I see." He seemed to nod in understand before snorting. "In that case, I only ask that you return home. I met you here out of a favor to Marden; I don't think anything will come out of it."

"P-please wait!" Zenovia began to rise to her feet. "I'm aware this territorial dispute is an unfortunate misunderstanding on both sides! We can still talk this over!"

Sirgis sneered as he shook his head. "How strange. I recall you refusing to discuss this further when we requested you return our land… Not to mention, we've already resolved the issue."

"What…?" Zenovia was just about to ask what he was implying.

"—Might I join you?"

The door swung open, revealing a young girl. She looked familiar to Wein.

"Princess Tolcheila…?!"

The princess of Soljest, Tolcheila.

The young girl Wein had met in Soljest stood before them.

"I thought we might meet again soon. It's been a while, Prince Wein."

He didn't question why she was here. It was obvious Gruyere had a lot of faith in her. That was why he'd sent her to Delunio as a special envoy to halt any negotiations with Natra.

"Your passionate gaze makes me feel naughty..." She looked at Zenovia. "I see. So you're the huge idiot who fell into our trap."

"Wha—" Zenovia's cheeks stung red with embarrassment.

Tolcheila giggled. "An incompetent ally is a burden. Wouldn't you agree, Prince Wein?"

"......"

As Wein remained silent, Sirgis spoke up in exasperation. "Interrupting diplomatic negotiations is not appropriate, Princess Tolcheila."

"No need to be so formal. This concerns Soljest, too, you know. Why don't I share the news? The loaned land will be returned to Delunio once our army recovers it."

Zenovia's breath caught in her throat. Next to her, Wein nodded in understanding.

Delunio was profiting off the fight between Soljest—a source of aggression for years—and Natra—an up-and-coming threat. The two nations would crush each other without any intervention. And coming out with Marden territory would be an ultimate win for Delunio.

"You're exactly like King Gruyere. You're a wild child..." Sirgis trailed off. "But Princess Tolcheila is right. Soljest will procure our lands for us. Do you understand why there is no need for discussion?"

"Ngh...!" Zenovia grit her teeth.

The bond between Delunio and Soljest was strong. She couldn't spy any weaknesses between them, but she had to split them apart somehow. If she couldn't figure something out, the fate of Natra and Marden would be all her fault—

"Princess Tolcheila," Wein said, suddenly speaking up. "This is regarding your earlier question. I do not think Lady Zenovia is incompetent."

"Yeah? Of all things to say. This is a huge oversight on her part."

"I know firsthand." Wein smiled. "I know she's the type who will keep getting back up even when she's knocked down."

Zenovia couldn't immediately tell if he was encouraging or ridiculing her for becoming discouraged. Regardless, it sparked something in her heart just as it was about to give in.

I accept it.

She accepted she'd faced failure after failure. However, Wein was right: She had struck back at traitorous vassals, the enemy nation that destroyed her homeland, and even Wein, who tried to use her for everything she was worth.

That was why she had it in her. She could fight back against this odious man.

"—I understand what you're saying," Zenovia began as she steadied her breath and switched her brain into high gear. "However, Sir Sirgis, will you be able to pull it off?"

"Are you questioning whether Soljest will be able to take the land back?"

Tolcheila giggled. "Natra defeating our troops? You can't be serious. Or you're plain stupid." She turned to Sirgis. "You're more acquainted with Soljest than these two here. What do you think?"

"I would declare it impossible. Soljest would never lose." Sirgis reluctantly took her side. Considering the rocky history of their nations, it was inevitable.

Zenovia has been hoping for this.

"Exactly. The army of Soljest is powerful. It will likely defeat Natra with ease. But won't victory bring you to a standstill?"

"What?" Tolcheila gasped.

"I'm saying there's a chance the troops of Soljest will face no harm and gain more power."

Sirgis's eyes narrowed. The young princess looked taken by surprise.

Though he would welcome the destruction of the two nations, Sirgis didn't think that was realistic. But what if the situation became much more complicated than he'd hoped?

It would be bad for us if Soljest crushes Natra and expands their borders...!

Any suggestion that Natra could topple Soljest could immediately be shot down, but they couldn't deny the possibility that Soljest would win by a landslide.

"... It's worth considering." Sirgis nodded sternly. The ridicule on his face was gone.

Next to him, Tolcheila gave it some serious thought for a few moments before playfully shrugging her shoulders. "How deplorable. You sound like you're implying we'll throw our allegiance out the window once we defeat Natra."

"Am I wrong?" Zenovia fired back.

Tolcheila took it square on. "We value loyalty. I will not stand for false accusations of betrayal!" she shouted. "Besides, even if Natra did eliminate Soljest, wouldn't you attack Delunio next?"

"False accusations? Speak for yourself. If we can resolve our differences, Natra is prepared to forge an alliance with Delunio."

It was a verbal battle between Zenovia and Tolcheila.

Sirgis watched on. "Excellent arguments... But Soljest has already promised to return our land. This is key."

There it is, thought Zenovia. She understood this well. That was why she had only one thing left to say.

"We'll hand over...twice the size of the original land."

"What was that...?!" Tolcheila's eyes widened.

Sirgis looked at her with interest. "Are you fine with that?"

Obviously not...! Zenovia barked silently but nodded with composure.

She would give up territory that she'd never intended on relinquishing. It was a huge step backward. It would hurt their economy and their military power. She'd lose popularity among her people, and it would hurt Natra's position.

But...! Despite it all, I want to take away their moral justification to fight and stop the invasion! That's the priority, even if it means I pay the price!

She was so stressed, she thought her heart might stop beating. In fact, that would have given her some respite, but she didn't want it to happen. She had to bear the weight of her decision.

"In that case, it is a different story."

"S-Sir Sirgis! Are you turning your back on our alliance?!"

"I wouldn't. However, it's not your place to decide whether we reconcile or not."

He sounded ready to abandon her. Tolcheila's eyes narrowed in annoyance.

You little rat! It's getting to your head! I need to delay their negotiation to give time for my father to crush their army...!

The gears in her mind were whirring.

Zenovia felt confident, just a little bit. Her hands balled into fists under the table.

All right—!

—*I win*, Sirgis quietly confirmed to himself.

He'd expected Zenovia to relinquish her lands for the sake of peace—and that Tolcheila would try to interfere.

Kids these days... No foresight, I tell you.

Sirgis's only concern was protecting his country from Soljest and Natra.

After Marden had become a vassal state, he'd predicted Soljest and Natra would team up. He had a hunch they would focus their attack on Delunio, which spurred him to find a way out.

His initial plan had been to form an alliance with Natra against Soljest, but it didn't take him long to reject this idea. Even if they tried to cooperate, he couldn't ever see them winning against Soljest. After all, he was basically traumatized by Gruyere's kingdom in the past.

Even if they did win, the damage would be astronomical. He couldn't care less about the deaths of hundreds of thousands of soldiers from Natra, but those of his own people were unforgivable. He would never let them die in a meaningless war. For this reason, Sirgis had chosen to ignore his official duties to pursue an alliance with Soljest.

I'm aware of King Gruyere's nature. He was planning to fight the crown prince all along.

That was why Sirgis had secretly negotiated with the king. If Gruyere wanted to fight with Natra, the prime minister would provide the moral grounds to wage war. In return, Soljest would take part of Marden territory and return it to Delunio.

In the end, they had reached an agreement. War had broken out between Soljest and Natra.

It must seem as if the two countries are about to crush one another…

But this wasn't true, of course. Sirgis was certain Soljest would be victorious. In his opinion, synchronized destruction was an impossibility.

Others wouldn't be able to follow his logic. After all, wouldn't that just give Soljest more power? The alliance would fall through with time. Even if Natra cut them down to size, Soljest would grow large enough to bare its fangs at Delunio.

Their theory was right. Of that, Sirgis was certain, which was why he had another plan.

When we get back our land…I'll donate it to Levetia.

The Kingdom of Marden had fallen to Cavarin in the previous year. There was no mistaking it had been a dirty move. Even so, they had received no criticism from foreign nations.

Why? Because the king had been a Holy Elite. In the West, it served as a pardon.

Even if Soljest attacks us, no one will come to our aid, just as we did not rush to Marden's side. But that will all change if we have a Holy Elite!

If Delunio could just get their hands on one, not even King Gruyere would be able to invade so easily.

I'll prolong this meeting to interfere with Soljest. That will only incite Natra's enmity. All eyes will be on us as the three nations wage war. And in the midst of it, I can lay the groundwork to donate this land…and become a Holy Elite!

The prerequisites to become a priest were arbitrary: experience as a priest, contributions to Levetia's cause, coming from the bloodline of the founder or his lead disciples, among others. The real task was gaining the support of the majority of the other members. That virtually canceled out every other condition. A large contribution would secure him some support.

A commoner becoming a Holy Elite! I'd be up there with the likes of King Gruyere!

That was the dream—sweet and tempting. He would become a Holy Elite—someone who could guide his beloved nation forward. One might say no greater glory could be found in this world.

We don't need new land! Our territory has a long and storied history! Our people are good and devout! We have a rich culture! Delunio is already perfect! If I were to become one of the holy few, it will only cement its perfection!

That vision was about to become reality. Now that he'd come this far, his plan was unstoppable.

Except Sirgis had forgotten…that there was another monster in the room.

Wein Salema Arbalest.

"It seems we have come to an agreement," Wein said suddenly, breaking the silence.

This snapped the prime minister back to his senses. "Prince Wein, do you have no objections to ceding part of Marden?"

Zenovia was lord of the territory, but Wein was her superior. They'd run into problems if he refused, but—

"It's Lady Zenovia's decision. I have nothing to add."

He gave his approval. He must have realized it would leave him at a disadvantage, but his expression gave away nothing.

"If you say so. Well then…"

"Yes," Wein agreed with a nod.

"Why don't we get down to *the real discussion*?"

What? They balked at him, except for Zenovia.

No one had any idea what he was talking about. They had just settled things between Natra and Delunio.

"Prince Wein, what do you mean by 'the real discussion'?" Sirgis couldn't help himself.

Wein flashed a smile at him. "—Let's go kill Gruyere together."

Gruyere looked out upon the standstill, appearing bored.

"Natra's defenses are persistent. They're not moving at all."

"Which is giving us a hard time."

Gruyere sighed at the one subordinate. "I say it's high time I make my move..."

"You can't! Have you forgotten their surprise attack?!"

"Exactly! They could be setting up a trap at this very second, waiting for us to charge our way through!"

"We ought to proceed with caution!"

Gruyere was stumped by the choir of protests. The enemy generals Raklum and Borgen had led a surprise attack that had targeted him. However, one could see from his overall health that they had failed. Gruyere's military prowess had enabled him to survive the attack. His soldiers had come rushing to his aid, forcing the enemy generals to retreat.

Though he had ordered his men to hound them, the generals had slipped away as the soldiers fretted over his welfare. The army had tightened their formation around him, which meant their offensive attacks were lacking. This prevented them from breaking through the enemy army. A few days had already passed since they fell into a deadlock.

That surprise attack got me all excited, but I never thought it would leave me caged in...

Gruyere glanced up at the sky. Evening was already upon them. The sun would soon set and fade to night, making it impossible to engage in any battle.

Well, no big deal. All my men are growing impatient. If tomorrow seems boring, I'll beat Natra down with the weight of my entire army.

He was about to order his generals to pull back their army...

"Hmm—?"

Under his gaze, Gruyere witnessed the enemy troops making their move.

"...I don't get it," Sirgis said to Wein in a serious voice. "Killing King Gruyere... Why would I agree to doing that?"

The prime minister must have not wanted to cause any discord, because his refusal was polite. If he entertained Wein's stupid proposal, it threatened to ruin their agreement.

Wein flashed him a teasing smile, looking carefree. "Why? Don't you want to kill the king?"

—You imbecile! I would have done that a long time ago if I could have pulled it off! Sirgis shouted inside.

If presented the chance, he would kill Gruyere in a heartbeat. Ever since Sirgis became prime minister, he couldn't count how many times the king caused him grief.

Even so, it was impossible. Gruyere was stronger than the average man. On the battlefield, the mere mention of his name made officers and soldiers of Delunio tremble.

"Please stop joking around. If you refuse to let it go, I'll have no choice but to reconsider our agreement!" His tone grew gruff.

Half of it was a performance and half from the heart. His experience as prime minister told him these conversations could turn dangerous if allowed to continue.

"...I believe Lady Zenovia mentioned this earlier, but..." Wein started, suddenly changing topics. "I'm concerned about Soljest winning by a landslide. If that happens, civilian lives will be involved. As prince, that would break my heart."

"......" Sirgis couldn't help but feel confused.

What's with this boy? What's he trying to say...?

He couldn't get a read on him. Was he moving the conversation forward with something else in mind?

Sirgis glanced at Zenovia and saw the anxious look on her face.

She seemed to know what he was implying. However, he couldn't guess from her expression alone.

"...It's no wonder they call you a benevolent ruler, Prince Wein."

Sirgis had to try to figure it out on his own. He went on.

"Your people are your priority. I understand. Although I cannot come together with you to form a joint front against Soljest... I would be willing to accept those seeking refuge."

How's that? Sirgis awaited his response.

The previous deal would have left Delunio as the sole winner. Wein was trying to get him to pay the price, albeit a small one.

If he agrees to this, we'll be fine. But if he comes out with any more surprises...

There was a good chance they would have to reconsider their deal.

Wein nodded. "That would be very helpful. My people would be relieved. Are you sure? I know Delunio isn't very welcoming to outsiders."

"I admit we have a conservative stance to protect our culture. However, we are open enough to accept those who are displaced by the ravages of war."

Sirgis seemed to guess correctly: Wein wanted both parties to pay the price. The prime minister let out a sigh of relief.

"Well then," the prince said, "I'll be sure to send them your way—eight hundred thousand of them to be exact."

Sirgis's vision went white.

Eight hundred thousand. Tolcheila ruminated on that number in her mind.

Eight hundred thousand. That was around their current population, including Marden.

She could see through his scheme. Wein was insisting Delunio take in his entire kingdom.

"—What in the world are you saying?!" Tolcheila blurted out. "Accepting your entire population?! That's impossible! Why would you even suggest that?!"

"Why? You know, Princess Tolcheila." Wein smiled. "Natra is on the brink of collapse. Isn't it my duty to consider the citizens' safety?"

"What?! On the brink of c-collapse?!"

Wein nodded dramatically. "The enemy army is powerful. You were right about that. I'm certain we'll be defeated and they'll close in on the capital with ease. That's why I wanted to find a place for my people to flee beforehand… Isn't that a perfectly normal reason?"

Tolcheila was at a loss for words.

It did make sense, but she didn't understand it. How could she ever comprehend something that would devastate their own countries?

"Th-that's…preposter…"

"Don't be ridiculous!" Sirgis blurted next to Tolcheila as she trembled. "A few hundred or a thousand is one thing, but eight hundred thousand?! No way we can accommodate them!"

"I agree," Wein replied with a nod. "But we're going to send them anyway."

"Nnghhh… Damn it! Are you out of your mind?!"

Rage was turning his face all kinds of colors.

"We'll use military force to keep them out! We'll show no compassion or mercy! Thousands of civilians will die without ever entering our borders! Is that what you want?!"

Sirgis wasn't bluffing. If that came to pass, he would make sure to see it through. The prime minister saw foreigners as dust. The people of Delunio were the only real treasure.

However, Wein was steadfast.

"Defending yourself through force? …Is your army capable of that?"

"What…?!" His eyes widened. He could instinctively tell Wein wasn't spouting whatever came to his head.

But what could keep the military from functioning?

As Sirgis furiously turned it over in his mind, Wein flashed him a grin.

"Don't you think yellow stands out?"

Everyone in the room froze at this random statement.

"Yellow? Yellow…"

Something was tugging at Sirgis. Memories of yellow clothes flooded his mind. He questioned why he was remembering this now, and—

"…Damn it…!" He came across a likely answer. "Was that why you chose that gaudy color? To stir our youth and spark an internal rebellion?!"

This shocked Tolcheila. *I remember seeing some kids in yellow on the way here.*

Why would that sow the seeds of rebellion?

Wein glanced at Tolcheila as she came up empty.

"Out of all colors…red, blue, black, white…yellow clothes are at the bottom of the barrel. The color is just too bright to be incorporated into an outfit. In fact, it makes you stick out like a sore thumb."

Products made in Natra were all the rage in Delunio. Yellow outfits were being flaunted everywhere. High visibility was helping the trend grow.

"By wearing the same color, it's fostered a sense of unity—as a group."

"Ah…" Tolcheila gasped.

What if they had a collective goal? Like rejecting conservation culture, for instance? Or defying a repressive religion? Or denouncing the nobility, who loved to gain concessions?

What if banding together as a group sparked anger and dissatisfaction, and the young people realized they needed to purge these things from their lives?

The youth are the cause of unrest! Yellow clothing has turned into their symbol, and they have started to rally under it like blistering flames!

It was an indescribable situation. Tolcheila shivered at this concept beyond all imagination. It was impressive she didn't break down. The average person would have found themselves in over their heads.

And Sirgis wasn't average.

"...Don't you dare look down on me, Wein Salema Arbalest!"

He banged his fist against the desk. Even though he accepted that he'd been unwittingly roped into this sneaky strategy, he would not fold his cards here.

"So what if a bunch of kids rebel?! It's just a phase! Our army will have them under control in an instant and—"

"Yellow dye is hard to come by," Wein interrupted. "After all, there isn't much demand for it. It was hard to procure, even from the Empire. And it has one pesky little trait."

He took a breath.

"It's made from a poisonous flower."

"Excuse me...?" Sirgis's mind ground to a halt.

What did he just say?

"Its poison is very potent, though the color payoff is subtle. It was originally meant for very small items, not clothes. When worn, it slowly weakens the body and eventually leads to death."

"W-wait... That can't be... There can't be something that convenient."

"Reports of people growing sick… Haven't you heard the reports?"

Sirgis looked appalled. He thought back to the reports from his subordinate a few days earlier. The phenomenon was among them.

"Sorry, Sirgis. Stirring up a rebellion is only the first step." Wein looked at the prime minister and grinned. "My plan is to destroy your youth once you've exhausted yourself from suppressing a rebellion."

"D-damn it! You…"

"Allow me to walk you through it. Your forces will mobilize to stop the uprising, but the youth will put up a tough fight. Well, I'll do my best to set it up that way. As soon as the suppression starts and body count increases, young people will drop like flies. There will be rumors it's a curse or an epidemic, and even the military will lose control of the subjects. They'll be racing to escape the country."

Wein went on. "That's when eight hundred thousand of my people will advance on you. The army will have no way to stop them. The people will start building villages first, then towns, and finally cities. They'll try to create a new life for themselves. The increase in population will result in a food shortage and cause cities to stagnate. The culture will become virtually unrecognizable, and the impoverished people of Delunio will try to reject my subjects. Naturally, we'll resist, causing disputes to break out and deteriorate public order. Surrounding nations will intervene under the pretext of aiding the refugees, who have been treated unjustly. Without a proper army of its own, Delunio will be immediately be invaded by foreign nations—"

Wein gave a troubled grin.

"Oh dear. It seems your kingdom will collapse."

* * *

He's a monster... Zenovia had thought when Wein told her about the plan a day prior.

"First, we'll go with your plan to cede the territory. If we can reach an agreement, then that's fine. After we form a real alliance with Gruyere and use my plan to get Delunio to destroy itself from the inside out, Soljest and Natra will take over."

Wein continued. *"Sirgis might pretend to go along with our plan to buy time. In that case, I'll intentionally reveal my plan to him, take Delunio itself hostage, and use both our countries to subjugate Soljest... Either way, Natra will come out on top."*

Zenovia had shivered.

He was basically saying they would threaten Delunio—by using Wein's own kingdom as a means to an end if it meant destroying Sirgis's beloved country. It was abnormal. How could royalty come up with this idea?

No... Prince Wein is the only one who could have concocted this plan.

Nobility considered themselves special, only because they were "noble." Because they were born "special" and carried "special" blood. Because it was only natural they would think this way.

However, Wein was different. On this continent, he must have been the only one who referred to his citizens as accomplices and snubbed his lineage. Only he could ever hit upon such an idea—even if it meant making a pawn of his ancestry and homeland.

"Q-quit...pulling my leg!" Sirgis shrieked, straining his vocal cords. "What the hell are you doing?! Do you think I'll put up with this? You bastard! How could you do this as a prince?!"

Wein had approached this with a vastly different point of view. Sirgis couldn't wrap his head around it. His ranting was all over the place.

"I—I know. I'll order the people to stop wearing your clothes immediately and…"

"Ha-ha-ha… Sir Sirgis. Do you think I'd be explaining this to you if I thought you could put a stop to it?"

"……Ngh!" Sirgis trembled. Anyone could see he was on the verge of breaking.

Tolcheila stepped in. "Pull yourself together, Sir Sirgis! You mustn't be fooled by his tricks! It's all hypothetical!" Her grin feigned concern, as she glared at him. "I have never heard of such a dye! Even if people have fallen ill, it could be coincidental!"

"Look into my eyes, Princess Tolcheila. Do I look like I am lying?"

"Obviously!"

"Ouch. That's not nice." Wein shrugged his shoulders.

But she's not wrong!

As the princess pointed out, there was no such dye. Even if it did exist, there was no way they'd cultivate a dangerous plant in large quantities. Everything about the poison was a bluff.

The uptick in illness was no coincidence.

By dressing themselves in our shoddy clothes, they're basically wearing close to nothing as the season is turning. Of course they're going to get sick.

Natra's inferior industries weren't anything new, but only the citizens were in the know. Sirgis and Tolcheila were none the wiser.

Either way, Wein had already driven the stake through his heart. Anyone could see Sirgis was panicking. Tolcheila could still express her suspicions, but the prime minister was about to spiral. The princess understood that arguing over whether the dye was poisonous wouldn't help Sirgis make a comeback. She approached it from a different angle.

"You almost got me, Prince Wein! If I had nothing to do with this matter, I would have planted a kiss on your lips! Let's say you managed to bring unrest to Delunio. Is it even feasible to bring eight hundred thousand people here?"

It just sounded reckless. It would include women. Children. The elderly. The sick. Those who were eager to go west. Those who wanted to hold on to their connections to the Empire. It seemed impossible to lead them as a collective...

"But didn't I pull it off with *thirty thousand people*?"

A shiver went up their spines.

Right... Prince Wein has done this before! He managed to mobilize the citizens of Mealtars!

Of course, it was no eight hundred thousand. It was hard to say if his skills would transfer to a larger crowd. However, even with the entire decimal point difference, he had succeeded in mobilizing thirty thousand people, which was an impressive feat by itself.

"In that case... I know! I'll take your head...!" Sirgis bellowed, shaking his fist.

"You've misunderstood me. Falanya was the one who pulled it off. I just supported her. I've already given her detailed instructions to mobilize if I die here... So, what will you do?"

"Ngh...AAAAH!" Sirgis hung his head powerlessly, keeping his fist in the air.

"I need to stop my father from invading...!" Tolcheila persisted doggedly. "Your strategy will only work if we're hostile. Without a true threat, your subjects won't be up in arms, even if you insist as prince and princess. It'll buy us time to come up with a new strategy with Delunio!"

"—Pardon me!" An official dashed through the doors.

"What the hell is it?! Can't you tell we're busy?!" Tolcheila took out her irritation on him.

"But I have an urgent message for Sir Sirgis..."

The prime minister looked up.

"Spit it out already! If it turns out to be nothing, I'll kick the shit out of you!"

"Y-yes!" He wasn't sure why a foreign princess had rebuked him. "We received news on the battle between Natra and Soljest. The contents read—"

"Reporting in! The troops of Natra have abandoned their post and retreated. It has been confirmed they're heading toward a fortress in the mountains! It seems a flying column had been putting it together! At this rate, we believe the two troops will converge!" reported the scout.

The commanders led by Gruyere groaned in unison.

"They got us..."

"I guess that surprise attack was just to buy time?"

"I think they were hoping to get His Majesty's head if the opportunity presented itself. But they'd always had a backup plan."

The other day, Gruyere's army had upped their defenses after receiving reports that their enemy was moving around sunset. With poor visibility, nighttime battle spelled friendly fire. After being ambushed, the top leaders of his army were naturally wary of a night raid. They chose to raise up an impregnable wall with the king at its center.

As a new day dawned, the army was met with an astonishing sight. The enemy camp was completely deserted. They had hurriedly scouted the four corners, when they received news of an eyewitness report.

Their army of eight thousand had suffered no major causalities, managing to keep Soljest at bay for days before abandoning their camp in the night. It was like they were mocking their hypervigilance. They'd escaped to a fortress they'd stealthily set up behind them.

"They're just buying time."

"Indeed. There haven't been major casualties on our side either. Even if they lock themselves away, they have a long way to go before they can hope to match our men. We can't be careless, but there is nothing to fear."

"Turning tail at the eleventh hour? And they call themselves soldiers? They're choosing a path that welcomes criticism from society. What a disgrace."

They weren't bluffing. Soljest still had the upper hand, even if Natra had duped them. The generals knew this, so morale remained high…all except for Gruyere.

His expression was stern. *Something feels off…*

The enemy was buying time. It certainly seemed that way. However, he couldn't help but feel like he was missing something. He could feel an indescribable sensation settling in his gut.

But this is part of the fun.

Gruyere smiled. The real thrill was not in a one-sided hunt, but the rush of risking your life on the battlefield. His heart began to pound. He could feel something burning inside him.

"Tell all the forces: We're chasing our escaped prey."

"""Yes!"""

The officers responded in unison.

"—General Hagal!"

Hagal had ordered the fortress to be built. He turned around.

Raklum and Borgen stood behind him on horseback.

"It seems you're doing well. I'm glad we could meet up again."

"I apologize for the trouble. I return full command of the army to you, General," Raklum replied.

"Yes… So tell me. How was King Gruyere on the battlefield?"

"Beyond our expectations. He was even able to repel my arrows." Borgen shrugged.

"The surprise attack plan was a success, though I'm ashamed to report I couldn't slay him." Raklum had some pent-up frustration.

Hagal nodded. "That's just the way it is. It's near impossible to take down big game in one shot. I won't tell you to get over it, but our next battle is just up ahead. Getting caught up in the past will dull your sword."

"Right..."

"Besides, everything is still progressing according to plan. The enemy has assumed we're retreating to buy time," Hagal stated.

Borgen looked at the troops of Soljest heading toward them. "Do you think those guys have realized the prince's true aim?"

"Absolutely not," Hagal replied, remembering how Wein had given his orders. "There's no way. His ideas are too far removed from any soldier hoping for victory."

Hagal's voice seemed to house both fear and admiration.

"Who else would factor in the retreat of their own army to the diplomacy schedule?"

"The armies have clashed, and Natra has turned tail...!"

As they listened to the official's report, the victor—Tolcheila—gulped. Her ally, Sirgis, moaned.

"Wow! Your troops never let me down! Very strong!"

The loser—Wein—seemed to be more confident than anyone else and smiled.

"At this rate, Soljest will soon descend upon the capital. Oh no, Princess Tolcheila," he said. "It seems we've run out of time to talk."

"W-wait...! Please give me the details of your troops' retreat!"

"I'm terribly sorry. We don't know much yet… But your troops are in pursuit."

"Ngh…!" Tolcheila gritted her teeth.

It was hard to get precise details from the front lines. It took time for news to trickle in, and those on the field wanted to report as much good news as possible.

We haven't withdrawn. We've just fallen back after a little scuffle. But I knew they would convey it that way in the initial report.

Everything was going according to his calculations, which he had settled prior to heading for Delunio.

Wein took everything into account: the rate of advance of their respective armies; the date, time, and location of their projected battlefield; its distance to the capital of Delunio; the speed of the horses; their diplomatic itinerary. There was nothing he missed. He even planned for the initial report to arrive that day.

I didn't think the timing would be so perfect!

After all, Sirgis had been driven into a corner. If Wein was going to question him, this was the time to do it.

"Sir Sirgis, I understand your feelings," Wein said sadly. "At this rate, Delunio will be ravaged by rebellion and broken apart by my eight hundred thousand subjects. The remaining people of Delunio will lose their country, culture, and pride, leaving them no choice but to be nomads. It's a cruel state of events. My heart goes out to you."

"…Shut up, devil!" Sirgis screeched in his bloodcurdling manner. "You think I'll stand for this?! Do you think nothing of your own subjects?"

"Of course, I trust and value them. I think they'll walk down their own paths, regardless of their geographic location."

Out of context, he sounded like a benevolent ruler who adored his people. However, he was implying he was destroying his own country *because* he trusted his citizens. He was playing in a whole different dimension.

That's impossible! Sirgis's heart panged.

He prided himself on his love for his country, culture, and people. He believed anyone involved in politics shared this sentiment. This was why he couldn't imagine coming up with this plan and executing it.

There's no way! Tolcheila tried to pray away her agitation.

She had been trained in military affairs. She knew it wasn't realistic to pass an edict on eight hundred thousand people and guide them all to safety in a single nation.

It might have been possible if they were trained soldiers. However, they were eight hundred thousand average citizens. Leading them would be a complete nightmare.

It was out of the question. It had to be. No doubt.

"*—I'll do it.*"

The two caught their breath. The boy sitting before them emanated dreadful power.

Their hearts wavered. Their confidence diminished. They had no choice but to feel he could pull it off.

Say it! Say it won't happen! I will be a Holy Elite! I will *guide this nation and its people!*

Sirgis opened and closed his mouth, willing himself to speak, but the only thing that came out was an awkward groan.

Wein whispered to him, "By the way, I have an antidote."

The prime minister gasped.

"Don't let him to take advantage of you, Sir Sirgis! The poisonous dye is a fabrication! You must not allow him to trick you with a fake antidote!" Tolcheila insisted.

Sirgis was too exhausted to hear her words.

An antidote. It would save the people. It was a ray of light that shined at the end of the tunnel. How could he resist? It didn't matter if the beacon of light came from the enemy's lamp in a tunnel of his own design.

"...What can I do to get it?"

"Sir Sirgis!" Tolcheila screeched.

Wein remained unfazed. "Though it might seem my men have withdrawn, they've already regrouped. I imagine they're engaging in combat right now."

The prince knew his army was holed up in the fortress, but this made it seem like Sirgis had a grace period.

"I want your army to launch an attack from behind. If Natra and Delunio get them in a pincher attack, Soljest won't stand a chance."

Tolcheila spoke up. "Wait! That would go against our alliance! No other nations would trust ever Delunio!"

"Th-that's..." Sirgis seemed uncertain.

It was not an easy decision to go against an international promise—against Gruyere, at that. To Sirgis, the king was a symbol of fear. He didn't want to turn his back on him.

"But think of your nation," Wein said, cutting into his thoughts. "You only have two options: Watch Soljest destroy Natra and see Delunio collapse under the weight of my subjects, or take down Gruyere together and form an alliance with Natra."

It was time to ask the final question.

"So, what will you do?"

Silence filled the room. Tolcheila clenched her teeth. Zenovia quivered with anxiety. Sirgis scowled.

A few moments passed before the prime minister spoke.

Several days had passed since the two armies started to move into the next stage of their battle.

To put it simply, the men of Natra were on the verge of collapse.

"General Hagal! The enemy has broken through the second line of defense!"

"Send out Finn's unit. Move Izali's and Lauro's units to fill in the gaps."

"Elnan's unit in the left flank is requesting reinforcements! The enemy attacks aren't showing any signs of slowing down!"

"And our traps?"

"We've already used them up…!"

"Roland, lead a hundred-man relief unit. I'll have other instructions for you after that."

"Understood!"

Hagal groaned as he gave out orders from the innermost part of the fortress.

Even though we're up against some major disadvantages, I didn't think we'd be cornered in…especially since we have this simple but sturdy structure.

He had expected their army to be skilled, but not by this much. The battle seemed to highlight their abilities. Their perfect synchrony seemed capable of even piercing through the ocean.

They've already broken past our first line of defense. We can't realistically hope to recover it.

Looking down below, he could see the enemy soldiers trying to rush up the mountain fortress, as his soldiers desperately attempted to hold them back.

It was only a matter of time before they fell. The truth was, Hagal knew it, too. They needed to come up with something soon.

I knew this would happen before the fight even began. General Hagal wasn't upset.

My duty is to buy time and watch over Gruyere…as our units put up a good fight.

His eyes turned toward the flanks of the enemy army lined up at the foot of the mountain.

There, he saw two cavalry units donning armor from Natra.

"Damn it! I never should have agreed to this…!" Borgen spat.

He had left behind the fortress and Hagal, sprinting around the plains as he led his cavalry. Their purpose was to interfere with Soljest.

"Look at their numbers. They can penetrate through our formation. We'll be overrun if we relegate ourselves to defense. Raklum, Borgen, lead a raid unit against the enemy to get their vitals," Hagal had ordered at the end of the first day.

Raklum and Borgen had nodded in silence. It was painfully obvious this was the truth. Soljest was just that strong.

"Captain! There's a hole in the enemy formation!"

"I know! All hands, follow me!"

The enemy defense wasn't as tight as their offensive strategies, which required intense focus.

With their cavalry units, Raklum and Borgen were to repeatedly look for gaps in the enemy formation. They rushed in at every opportunity, creating a disturbance before retreating. This took Soljest's attention away from offensive action.

Though easy to explain, the execution was nigh impossible.

General Hagal has lost his damn mind!

To be swift, each unit had five hundred men. This wasn't enough to crush their army of fifteen thousand, of course. On the contrary. If the enemy redirected their focus on them, Raklum and Borgen would be totally annihilated.

However, Soljest wouldn't do that. They wanted to topple the fortress and keep their energy focused on the army within its confines. They did the bare minimum to keep the two units at bay. They didn't go out of their way to pursue them, focusing on the castle as soon as the cavalry escaped beyond reach.

The two units continued to buzz around the army, like pests to distract them. However, if they crossed a line, Soljest would take them down pronto.

In other words, it was the cavalry's duty to risk their lives—irritating Soljest enough to keep them distracted, while not invoking the wrath of fifteen thousand men.

They calculated where to land their blows and when to retreat, jabbing their enemy with swords and arrows. This was in addition to reading into the enemy mindset and taking stock of their own men and horses. It felt like their brains were going to explode from going into overdrive. And if they failed, instant death. That was a fun bonus, right?

If they could, they would abandon their posts in a heartbeat.

We'll lose if we quit now. But we're just heading toward a slow defeat. It's almost funny.

Borgen scanned the battlefield.

We're supposed to buy time, but we might not be able to accomplish that. We need a way to turn the tide or...

He sensed activity from the enemy army.

—Brute force, huh.

Raklum clicked his tongue as he observed these new developments.

Soljest was trying to take the fortress by storm. They had kicked it up a few notches. Having switched all resources away from defense, they swooped down on Natra, massacring their soldiers. Natra resisted, concentrating their troops to take down the enemy, but it didn't change the situation. Instead of taking their time and keeping damage to a minimum, they had nosedived into a mountain of corpses and secured their imminent defeat.

At this rate, they'll reach the stronghold! What do we do—?!

With his eyes, Raklum scoured the battlefield in search of his best option.

And he found something he could work with.

"Ngh." Hagal groaned from the top of the fortress as he got a look at the full picture.

He stared down at the battle unfolding below for a few more beats before speaking to the adjutant next to him.

"I have to go. I'll leave you in command for now."

"Understood!" The adjutant nodded without hesitation. "But where, General?"

"Where these old bones are needed, of course."

The target was Gruyere.

Although Raklum's and Borgen's units were moving independent of each other, they miraculously aimed for the same place.

At this point, they couldn't care less if they pissed off the enemy. Going after the big catch was necessary if they wanted to stop Soljest. Gruyere was in the central rear. Now that his army had switched to raw force, the troops around him were sparse.

The situation was a rehash of their other surprise attack—except his time, they would succeed. They were unrelenting, converging their units and closing in on Gruyere at the back of the formation.

That was when the enemy soldiers at the rear pivoted, flipping back to look them in the eye.

"What?!"

"This is...!"

Raklum and Borgen couldn't believe their eyes.

The enemy units from both sides of the king had swiveled behind them, rushing toward the men of Natra as if to hold them in a suffocating embrace.

We were lured in—!

I was baited—!

It was not an improvised stunt. It was a premeditated trap. The two generals came to that same conclusion, synchronously calculating their next steps: Withdraw before the enemy completely surrounded them, or push their way forward to Gruyere?

However, neither had to make that choice. Before they had a chance, Gruyere was leading his cavalry toward them.

"You thought you would fool me twice? Big mistake!"

Gruyere's chariot closed in on Borgen, who instantly readied his spear. As soon as they crossed paths, the general's weapon crashed into the king's halberd, and he was thrown from his horse.

"*BORGEN!*" Raklum screamed, but Gruyere didn't give the fallen man another thought. He continued to drive his chariot at full force, this time toward him.

"Worry about yourself, General!"

Gruyere swung his halberd, which whistled through the air. It was the embodiment of violence, an attack that couldn't be avoided or deflected.

What could he do? Herculean strength could only be matched with raw power.

"RAAAAAAAGH!"

Raklum roared, engaging every muscle in his body. His strength was channeled into his gripped sword as he met the halberd head-on. Metal shrieked against metal. He could feel it ringing in his heart. Any witnesses would have noticed cracks running through the crossed sword and halberd.

"Well, well, well! Not bad!" Gruyere broke into a savage grin as he ran past Raklum and pivoted his chariot around.

The general was getting ready to go again, waiting to counter. His face had twisted into a grimace.

"Gah…!"

He looked down at his one arm. Pins and needles shot through it.

Can I counter with this arm…?

He shot down his own question. He had to, if he didn't want to die. This was no time to whine. He prepared himself, glaring at the king barreling toward him.

Taking advantage of the king's redirected focus, Hagal's unit appeared beside Gruyere.

"——Naargh!"

Gryuere's split-second reaction was impressive. A side sweep of his halberd could smash a boulder, severing the head of Hagal's horse as it tried to close in on him.

"…Tch!"

Gruyere clicked his tongue once, giving up on Raklum and leading his forces away. The general couldn't even process it, but when he saw Hagal on his knees next to the fallen horse, he rushed over.

"General Hagal!"

"He only got my horse. It's of no importance." He swung his sword to whip off the blood. "Take Borgen and get out of here. We've kept a gap open in their formation for a siege."

"U-understood!"

With Raklum in the corner of his eye, Hagal looked southwest.

"It's almost time…which means our next move is…"

"I meant to take him down with the horse, but…that was impressive."

Gruyere looked down at his arm as he maneuvered the chariot. He was bleeding.

Hagal had leaped from his horse, slicing Gruyere's arm as he flew over the king's head. He couldn't help but admire his acrobatics.

"Your Majesty! Are you injured?!"

"I will see to it right away!"

"Quit fussing. It's just a scratch."

His mind was churning even as he rebuked his subordinates. Should he go after that general again, or should he attack the fortress while their leader was away?

He looked around him as if in search of a clue…when he noticed something.

"…That can't be…"

From the southwest corner of the battlefield, he saw armed troops raising their flag high.

It was the flag of Delunio.

"Looks like we made it on time."

The army of Delunio had close to ten thousand soldiers. Accompanying them was Wein, who murmured to himself as he looked over the battle.

"I think our main forces are safe," Ninym responded next to him. "Did we need to rush with these troops, Wein?"

"We'd be back on square one if we found our men decimated. With Hagal holding fort, I wasn't too worried."

Wein went on. "Now that it's come to this, Soljest has no more moves. We've won."

The generals of Delunio gave the order to attack their enemy.

"Wh-what's that?!"

"Delunio?! Why are they here...? This can't be happening!"

"There looks to be about eight thousand soldiers... Maybe more!"

"This is an order for all units! There is a new enemy to the southwest! Rear guard! Defense formation! Stat!"

"Reporting in! Natra is sallying from the fortress! The front lines are requesting reinforcements!"

"Grr! They have to be working together!"

The subordinates were starting to realize what was going on, barking out orders.

Gruyere seemed euphoric, murmuring to himself. "—Marvelously done, Prince."

Why was Delunio here? It was obvious. Wein had persuaded Sirgis to deploy his men.

Gruyere wasn't sure how he'd pulled it off. And who could blame the king? If Gruyere had thought he could convince Sirgis, he would have done it first—but the king had thought nothing would sway him.

However, Wein found a way.

He had managed to coerce the petite man. It would have been great to see the prime minister bow before a teenage boy. It was too bad Gruyere couldn't have seen it for himself.

His subordinates were calling out to him.

"Your Majesty! It's unsafe here!"

"They'll corner us! We must evacuate immediately!"

"No enemies occupy the North! We can escape if we leave now!"

They all looked strung out. After all, they had been pincered by ten thousand soldiers.

All...except for Gruyere.

"Withdraw? What are you talking about? Do you think we've lost?"

"Ah, no, that's...well..."

"Don't be stupid. This is just the beginning," Gruyere assured, raising his voice. "Soldiers of Soljest! Fangs of your great king! Heed my voice!"

Over the metallic clash of swords and anguished cries, his beastly howl rang through the battlefield.

"Our army will go through hell if it means finding a way for survival! Do not lose yourself! Do not doubt yourself! Do not hesitate! If you succeed, glory will be ours!"

He sucked in a single breath.

"All units, follow me—!"

"It's over. Soljest will surrender any minute now."

In his stronghold in a back corner, Wein watched Delunio and Soljest make contact.

"Nice! Nice!" the prince commented, leaning back in his chair. "It'll be over soon. Well, I guess I still have to negotiate with them after the war. It's too soon to kick back. I guess I should contact Princess Tolcheila."

Ninym didn't take her eyes off the battlefield. "...Hey, Wein."

"Hmm? Did they surrender?"

"No." Something about her voice seemed fearful. "Soljest is coming this way."

"What?!" Wein snapped his head up and groaned. "This is...bad."

What do I do?

He knew what Gruyere was after, but Wein didn't have any cards lefts to play. Delunio wasn't under his command. They wouldn't heed his orders. Besides, there wasn't any time.

Should I run away for now...? But if I can't beat Gruyere here...

Wein's mind raced.

"There you are, Your Highness!" boomed one of his messengers, bowing before the shocked prince.

"I have an urgent message for His Highness from General Hagal!"

"Praise my name! Extol the name of your king! Let the enemy know we're here!" Gruyere yelled as he advanced forward, pushing his way through Delunio.

His men responded in turn, crying out their king's name, spurring Gruyere to prompt them again.

Delunio saw Gruyere as a bitter enemy, though he was a person to be feared. They would take him down if they could, but they also wanted to avoid coming face-to-face with him if they could help it.

Since Delunio had only just entered the battlefield, their hearts weren't ready. When it was announced they'd be up against Gruyere, their bodies had become paralyzed and their movements slowed. The king perceived this, forcing his way through in an ostentatious manner.

Natra and Delunio have never trained together. This is new to them. I doubt they're coordinated.

At most, they would only be able to work together well enough to attack the equipped soldiers of Soljest. If it broke out into a melee, he was dubious they would last very long.

That meant he had plenty of opportunities.

If we pierce through Delunio, their formation will block Natra from attacking us from the rear. If the two armies come into contact, it'll create chaos and slow their movements.

While the two armies were caught up with each other, Gruyere would consolidate his soldiers and pivot behind him—to crush the enemy commanders before they had a chance to pull themselves together.

For this to succeed, it necessitated a king to guide his soldiers, composed soldiers to follow orders in a high-risk situation, and skill. The Soljest army had it all.

I never expected Delunio to make a move! I'll give them that! But you're jumping to conclusions if you think you've won, Prince!

Far from disheartened, Gruyere led his forces with more excitement than ever—

Out of the corner of his eye, he caught sight of a hill to the left of his path. A large flag billowed there, marking someone standing right next to it.

The flag of Natra. Wein.

"——"

It's a trap, Gruyere's gut told him. He understood this, but he couldn't peel his eyes away.

He was consumed by greed. He could feel himself switching gears—from attacking the front lines to capturing Wein. It almost took the wind out of him.

"Taking the bait, Gruyere?"

The king felt like he could hear the prince, though it was physically impossible.

In that moment, an arrow pierced his right shoulder.

"Gwagh——?!"

Gruyere looked around—away from the hill on the left.

Torso wrapped in bloody cloth, General Borgen was standing a distance away with his bow poised at the king.

"I'll never be able to face the princess if I cannot take your head home with me…!"

Gruyere simultaneously caught sight of Raklum racing toward him on horseback.

"Don't think you'll get away, Gruyere!"

Sword against halberd. Gruyere tried to repel him, but his wounded arm throbbed, and there was excruciating pain radiating from his shoulder.

"RAAAAH!" Raklum swung his sword, knocking Gruyere off his chariot.

"Gah?!"

Drawing his attention in one direction to ambush him from the other. It was an incredibly simple tactic by itself. However, for it to work, they needed to correctly assume that he would try to break through enemy lines and get the jump on him. Using their own prince as a decoy was a bold move. Gruyere finally accepted he was dealing with a mastermind.

I need to make my escape—

This trap wouldn't spell the end. He regained his footing, switching his halberd over to his left hand, and observed...an old general standing before him.

"I made it on time." Hagal's sword glared. "Permission to be disrespectful?"

Gruyere paused for a moment before smirking. "Permission granted. There's no room for manners on the battlefield!"

His halberd ripped through the air.

Hagal's sword was far faster, lacerating his body.

It took only an instant for news of Gruyere's capture to spread through the battlefield.

The soldiers of Soljest started to cease their resistance and surrender, marking the end of their three-way war.

Epilogue

"—All right."

Wein stood in front of the door to a room, one fit for a noble.

One person was occupying it—their prisoner, Gruyere.

Though security was tight, he had been provided his basic necessities. After all, he was the king of a nation, so it wasn't as if they could toss him in the dungeon.

"Pardon me, King Gruyere."

When he stepped into the room, Wein was greeted by a single man.

"...Hmm?"

The prince scrunched up his face in confusion—and it wasn't because the man was voraciously devouring an array of food before him.

"...U-um, you're King Gruyere...right?"

"Hm? Oh, it's you. Long time no see."

He must have finally noticed Wein's presence. The man lifted his head, breaking into a composed smile. He sounded like Gruyere, but Wein wasn't completely sold. After all, there was no sign of his signature corpulence. Instead, he had the strapping physique of a hearty man.

"Um, you look like a whole new person..."

"Oh. Yeah, I'm skin and bones." Gruyere looked down at his own body.

His "gaunt" limbs and torso were sturdy. Even his face seemed more masculine.

"Because of my body type, I get reverted back to this state when I get injured or engage in strenuous activity. I find it irritating."

"……"

Hadn't there been a wound on his shoulder? Shouldn't there have been a gash on his arm? Gruyere was eating as if nothing had ever happened. Maybe fat had miraculous healing properties.

"How can I help you? Have you decided the date of my execution?" he asked while gnawing on a bone. "Are you going to decapitate or hang me or put me on the breaking wheel? You'll need some horsepower for the last one. Otherwise, I might come out in one piece."

"Oh, okay, I guess we can nix the last option then…Wait, I mean, we have no plans to take your head."

"Oh?" He seemed surprised. "If you get rid of me, Soljest will be yours. My son back home is no fool, but he is no match for you. Is Natra going to pass up an opportunity to rise up in power?"

"Nonsense. We had our reasons for crossing swords, but I've been hoping to forge a friendly relationship with you, King Gruyere, since the very beginning."

"Hmm…" Gruyere thought this over for a moment before grinning. "I see. You're afraid of causing trouble with Levetia."

"……"

Obviously, Wein thought.

Gruyere was one of the Holy Elite, the leaders of Levetia. If he was executed, they could expect backlash at the very least. In the worse-case scenario, it would spark all-out war. Wein wanted to avoid that if possible.

If we'd killed him with our surprise attack, we might have had a leg up in the grand scheme of things, but things wouldn't look pretty for us if we murdered him after a grueling war.

That had been why Wein had given orders to capture Gruyere alive if possible. Of course, anything could happen on the battlefield, which was why he had prepared himself for the worst.

"What would Delunio think if there's no execution?"

King Gruyere was their sworn enemy. Delunio had broken their alliance with Soljest to side with Natra. If Gruyere wasn't executed and Soljest remained intact, Delunio would have to sleep with one eye open, anticipating revenge.

"They'd think nothing of it. Delunio agreed the three nations should meet to discuss the future, even without your execution."

"That's surprising. I imagined Sirgis would have something to say about it."

"He was overthrown," Wein casually admitted.

The king blinked back at him.

"He had to give up his political career after crossing the line. After all, he acted in his personal interests to form an alliance with Soljest and break ties to join us."

"...I see." Gruyere snorted. "Two nations, two goals: Natra wishes to remain neutral to Levetia, and Soljest wishes for me to live. We've formed an involuntary team to drag Sirgis from his post."

Wein smirked. "I have no idea what you're talking about. Anyway, the new prime minister appears to be open to reconciling. He's advocating an alliance between the three nations. I expected this to happen, since new leaders tend to reject the ideas of their predecessors to form their own political platform."

He took out some documents, handing them to Gruyere.

"Sign this. Then we can prepare someone from Soljest to come get you. I imagine you're sick of living here. Feel free to return home."

Gruyere took the pen from Wein. He twirled it with his fingers—then snapped it in two.

"I think I'll die here after all."

"What?" The prince's eyes almost bugged out.

"I live as I please. I don't want my life to be dictated by the whim of others."

"P-please! Wait! That means…"

"It means Levetia might wage war. Ha-ha-ha! Oh boy! You have it in for you! And it won't affect me, 'cause I'll be six feet under!"

"Y-you little…!"

Gruyere was trying to land the final blow by memorializing his death as martyrdom.

He plays dirty, Wein thought.

"If you want me to return to my kingdom in one piece, I have a few conditions."

"…Which are?" Wein asked, feeling sick to his stomach.

Gruyere brought his face close to Wein's.

"Young prince, what is the true form of the beast you carry inside you?"

"…What beast?"

"Everyone has one. Call it 'desire' if you like. Yours is enormous, but I can't put my finger on it, which makes me very curious."

Gruyere went on. "Let it out. Say it. Show me the beast inside you. What is it after? Then I'll cooperate with your little meeting between the three nations."

"…"

Silence hung over them as they locked eyes.

It wasn't a display of animosity or malice. They were sizing each other up.

At long last, Wein started to give in. He let out a little sigh and told the king without hesitation.

"__________."

His voice was strained, but Gruyere hung on to every word.

"...Is it true, Prince?"

Sweat trickled down Gruyere's cheek. He lay waste to every threat on the battlefield, but this one statement made him crawl with apprehension.

"Believe me or not. It's up to you. I will say one thing: If you die here, you will never know the truth."

That threw the king off guard. He was quick to recover, hooting with laughter.

"Ha-ha-ha-ha! You've got me in checkmate! Very well! I admit defeat! I can't rot away here, now that I've heard about your goals!"

Gruyere flashed him a savage look. "I'll be waiting, Prince... Wein Salema Arbalest! Entertain me by wreaking havoc on the continent and coming out on the other side!"

"I don't know if I can provide much entertainment, but I think your people will be overjoyed that you aren't going to kill yourself. I certainly am. Here's another pen."

"Yes!" Gruyere took the new one, ready to sign the documents. "...Wait. What's with this ransom amount?"

"*Tch.* Didn't think you'd notice," Wein mumbled.

The king scanned over the documents again. They listed outrageous demands, including a ridiculous ransom fee and war reparations and the condition to hand over Soljest's harbor.

"You're ripping me off, Prince. Objectively speaking."

"What are you talking about? Asking for any less would be disrespectful to your name."

"Oh please. We're friends, right?"

"Which is why we need to bury any lingering resentment. With cash."

"No—"

©Falmarc

Until his people came to pick him up, Wein and Gruyere hemmed and hawed over the price.

"...Phew. That wraps up all loose ends concerning the war."

Zenovia put down her pen and sighed, having wrestled through the paperwork on her desk.

"I'm exhausted..."

She collapsed onto the desk.

Jiva collected the papers. "There was a point where I worried things would go south, but I'm happy they all worked out."

"Thanks to the vassals."

Zenovia had almost paid with her life for her oversight, which gave an advantage to Delunio. After further negotiations and the successful capture of Gruyere, they managed to settle things and escape censure. It offered the vassals some respite.

She continued. "Besides, we were able to buy back the land. Our losses were far less than expected."

Marden had ceded part of their territory to the other side, though it didn't take long for Delunio to propose selling it back for a reasonable price.

It was all the doing of their new prime minister. The loaned land had never had many natural resources. Even though it was on the pilgrimage route, it had only thrived under the rule of Natra, which allowed its residents to trade with the Empire. In other words, Delunio didn't have reason to stay fixated on it.

Besides, Delunio had to repair their relationship with Natra and Soljest as soon as possible. After all, they'd schemed to trick Wein's kingdom before betraying their coconspirators. By making enemies of two countries, their demise would be just around the corner if they did nothing.

To pacify Natra, they relinquished the land for an affordable price. They must have proposed something similar to Soljest, too.

"Prince Wein must have foreseen all of this."

Delunio should have been able to steal land from Natra with no effort, and yet they had come out of the battle empty-handed. Zenovia reflected on the dangers of diplomacy and Wein's natural aptitude for it.

But...I don't just want to accept I'm no match for him.

To Zenovia, Wein was a hero. This incident hadn't changed that. It only cemented the fact that they were worlds apart.

However, watching Wein's profile at the negotiation table, Zenovia realized something.

She wanted to catch up to him. She wanted to be recognized by him. She wanted her hero to accept her into his inner circle.

"By the way, Lady Zenovia, I've received some more marriage proposals for you. Your suitors must be taking this opportunity after hearing that your union with Prince Wein has fallen through."

"Refuse them all."

"Understood...Wait. Ah, I mean, that will be no issue, but..."

He never expected her to turn them down so quickly. Jiva observed her.

"...Lady Zenovia, did something about you change?"

Maybe it was the air about her. Or the way she carried herself. There was something about her, as if she had grown a spine.

"I don't think I've changed..." Zenovia smiled. "But I think I understand what I need to do."

The road ahead would be a tough one, but it was worth the effort.

If things went well... If he deemed her worthy... If that time ever came, she herself might propose to become his wife.

Zenovia ballooned with enthusiasm.

"—So."

Wein looked decidedly gloomy in his office. "I'll get straight to the point: Is our budget coming out net positive?"

"We're on thin ice."

"GAAAAAAH!" Wein let out a bloodcurdling shriek when Ninym handed down her verdict.

"The reparations covered the cost of war. Our partial rights to the harbor in Soljest are still an unknown variable. We didn't blow our budget out of the water by paying under the table to unseat Sirgis or buy back the land. I guess our biggest issue is King Gruyere. The followers of Levetia are keeping us at arm's length, which means fewer pilgrims are stopping in Marden."

These followers were the main source of their good fortune. By doing business with the pilgrims, it made others interested in Marden, creating a positive feedback loop and stimulating the economy. A decrease in their activity shared a direct correlation with an economic recession.

"That has slowed the boom in Marden. At least it's buying us time to deal with the economic gap between us."

"Except that means nothing if we're losing business!"

"Get over it. We can only wait for our reputation to recover with time."

"NOOOOO!" He clutched his head.

Ninym looked at him from the corner of her eye. "There is one more thing. We did gain something. Depending on your value system, you might say this is a net positive."

"Could it be…?"

Someone barreled through the doors.

"Are you done with your work, Prince Wein?!"

Before them was the princess of Soljest, Tolcheila.

"You must realize doors can be opened with a gentle push, Princess Tolcheila."

"Oh, but we have a custom of making an entrance. Guess I'm not accustomed to your culture. Forgive me."

She certainly didn't appear sorry as she flashed them a smile.

Why was Tolcheila here in Natra?

The answer was simple. She was an "exchange student"—basically, their hostage.

"It seems Tolcheila has taken a liking to you. I believe I will have her stay with you for a while as a hostage until the treaty is settled," Gruyere had proposed.

The story didn't end there.

"No hostage necessary. I trust you, King Gruyere."

"No need to hold back. Take her."

"...You're forcing her on me."

"...Our personalities are basically the same. I think it'll be hard to find her a husband when she's of age. But would you look at that! You're royalty, too! And a bachelor. I mean, I'll let Tolcheila's wiles guide you, of course."

"Please let me refuse your offer."

"Ha-ha-ha. I feel like dying for some reason. In fact, I'm going to slit my throat right now."

"Fine! I understand...!"

That was the gist of their conversation.

"And your answer to my question?" Tolcheila pressed.

Wein seemed reluctant. "Well, yes, I'm finished, but..."

"Would you like to enjoy a cup of tea outside? I just finished baking. I was very surprised by your customs. Your staff were shell-shocked to see a princess step into a kitchen!"

Tolcheila was a pushy one. It had been like this every day since she arrived. Wein felt like a small animal had grown attached to him. He didn't mind, but…

"Wein, may I come…*in*?!" someone yelped.

His sister, Falanya, froze as soon as she stepped in the room.

"Princess Tolcheila, *again*…?!"

"Oh, Princess Falanya, what a coincidence. We're just about to have a tea party. Could you save any business with him for later?"

"What, W-Wein?! You said you would spend time with me…!"

"Uh, well, that's…"

Though they were the same age, Falanya and Tolcheila couldn't seem to get along. They never missed a chance to pick a fight, especially his little sister.

Wein couldn't exactly disrespect his guest of honor. But it pained him to see his sister hurt. He looked at Ninym to save him from the situation…

You brought this on yourself. Deal with it.

Her face was blank as she stuck her nose in the air.

…*Sigh.*

Caught between the two girls, Wein immersed himself in his thoughts.

Please let me sell off this stupid kingdom and skip town forever!

His internal shriek rang in his ears for a long time, never reaching anyone's ears.

©Falmaro

Afterword

Long time, no see. It's Toru Toba.

Thank you for picking up this volume of *The Genius Prince's Guide to Raising a Nation Out of Debt (Hey, How About Treason?)*.

The theme is boss battles! The plot relies on Gruyere, the Holy Elite. Remember him? His first appearance was in the third volume. See him deal with Wein for yourself.

I have one piece of news I'd like to share.

This month will mark the beginning of the manga adaptation of this series on the *Manga UP!* app. I hope you'll check out your favorite characters on this new medium! I bought an iPad explicitly for this purpose, which means I'm one step closer to integrating into society, but it might take me a while to get the hang of it…

It's time for words of gratitude.

To my editor, Ohara. I'm sorry for missing my deadlines. I was only able to finish this volume with your support. Thank you. I'll do my best to finish my manuscripts on time!

To my illustrator, Falmaro. Thank you for your beautiful illustrations. The new designs are so nice! Love a character who's a little stubborn! It makes me want to write more scenes with her.

To my manga artist, Emuda. As the author and a reader, I'm

looking forward to the serialization. I'm excited to keep working with you!

Lastly, I would like to thank my readers. You're the reason this series is going strong. I plan to work even harder to meet your expectations—and be as good as the manga!

I'm hoping the next volume will be a little palate cleanser that focuses on daily life. Maybe some insight into different sides of Wein or his schoolboy days. But no promises!

At any rate, I'll try to write something good. Let's meet again in the next volume.

It's hard work taking it slow...

After living a painful life as an office worker, Azusa ended her short life by dying from overworking. So when she found herself reincarnated as an undying, unaging witch in a new world, she vows to spend her days stress free and as pleasantly as possible. She ekes out a living by hunting down the easiest targets—the slimes! But after centuries of doing this simple job, she's ended up with insane powers... how will she maintain her low key life now?!

IN STORES NOW!

Light Novel Volumes 1-7

Manga Volumes 1-3